Praise for Pr[...]

'I really appreciate the rang[...] ...bition on display in these stories. These are writers putting work into voice and craft rather than relying on event alone, and that's what makes their work persist in the mind.'

Chris Power

'One of the best multi-author short-story collections that I have read in recent years. The 2019 longlist achieved an impressive feat, demonstrating the variety and power of the form.'

Jarred McGinnis

'An illuminating and vivid range of stories from an exciting array of new voices already so accomplished in their craft.'

Sharmaine Lovegrove

'Full of verve, emotional enquiry and imagination. From atmospheric settings and distinctive images to stylish precision and exactitude, the multiple and intricate ways of seeing, feeling and thinking that can be found in these stories are invigorating.'

Harriet Moore

Brick Lane Bookshop
Short Story Prize

Longlist 2021

A Brick Lane Bookshop Publication

Designed, typeset and project-managed by Kate Ellis

First published by Brick Lane Bookshop in 2021

ISBN 978-1-91620-822-3

Brick Lane Bookshop
166 Brick Lane
London
E1 6RU

www.bricklanebookshop.org

A CIP record for this book is available from the British Library

Printed and bound in Great Britain by Clays Ltd, Elcograf S.p.A.

for short-story lovers everywhere

Contents

Foreword

Denise Jones

This is the third Brick Lane Bookshop Short Story Prize anthology and I hope you enjoy the selection of stories in our 2021 edition.

I was asked recently why Brick Lane Bookshop decided to run a short story competition alongside the many others in London. There are several reasons, past and present:

First, the bookshop has a history of publishing, which we are keen to continue. Second, we want to encourage new writers and promote their stories as widely as we can. Third, we want to establish a Brick Lane Bookshop publishing venture that will work on a variety of ideas for publications in the future.

We offer cash prizes and the inclusion of the longlisted stories in an annual printed anthology. This is our way of identifying new writers, disseminating their work and raising their profile. It's exciting to discover previously unpublished talent and gratifying to find that the Brick Lane Short Story Prize anthologies are popular amongst readers.

In this pandemic year, 2021, we received 734 entries, and warm thanks go to Kate Ellis, the coordinator of the project, for her patience, creativity and excellent organising skills –

and for reading all 734 stories! Thanks also to all the readers who sifted the submissions and gave their opinions, the Brick Lane Bookshop team for their untiring support, and this year's brilliant judges, Elise Dillsworth, Wendy Erskine and Kishani Widyaratna, who gave their time to agree the shortlist and decide the winners. Thanks too to everyone who entered their very varied stories; please keep on writing! Many congratulations to Aoife Inman for winning the first prize of £1,000 for her story 'Earth-Grown Bodies', to the runners-up, Danielle Vrublevskis and Katherine Gutierrez, and to all the longlisted writers who are published in this anthology.

Returning to my earlier reference to the bookshop's history of publishing, I'm proud of the fact that we were one of the founder members of the Federation of Worker Writers and Community Publishers (FWWCP), now renamed TheFED.[1] Brick Lane Bookshop, under its previous names of Tower Hamlets Arts Project (THAP) and then Eastside Books, with its associate Stepney Books, was a member of the FWWCP in the 70s and 80s. It was a network of community-based writing groups that stretched across the UK. Community-run groups met so that working-class people could share and discuss their creative writing and to facilitate community self-publication. Federation members believe it was the most significant working-class writing/publication project of the twentieth century, distributing over a million books between 1976 and 2007.

Many of the groups emerged out of local politics and campaigning. Some were involved in the establishment of

---

[1] https://blog.archiveshub.jisc.ac.uk/2016/05/03/federation-of-worker-writers-and-community-publishers-collection-at-the-tuc-library-london-metropolitan-university/

community bookshops, providing different combinations of bookshop, publisher, crèche, café and legal advice, such as Hackney's Centerprise, Newham Books and THAP, and many others throughout the UK. They were important in providing an outlet for FWWCP publications and frequently provided a meeting space for writers and adult-literacy groups.

You can find reference copies of the books at the TUC Library's collection of publications from the Federation of Worker Writers and Community Publishers.[2]

Through poetry, prose, fiction, biography, autobiography and local history, they document the changing experience, working lives and cultural history of working-class people. They focus on issues of local community, immigration, race/ethnicity, gender, mental health and sexuality – very similar themes to those in the book you are holding. Brick Lane Bookshop still has copies of many of the FWWCP's publications on sale.[3] The Brick Lane Bookshop Short Story Prize anthologies are bringing this important collection into the twenty-first century.

Denise Jones
Owner Brick Lane Bookshop Ltd
August 2021

---

[2] https://blogs.londonmet.ac.uk/tuc-library/2018/08/
[3] https://bricklanebookshop.org/online-shop/

Introduction

Kate Ellis

I noticed the other day that the pages of our first anthology are going yellow, as the leaves already are. When time is doing strange things, or feels as though it's concertinaing as it has over the last year or so, these visual markers are a comfort. In the introduction to the yellowed 2019 anthology, I wrote that 'we're celebrating the short story because that means celebrating ideas, creativity, curiosity and imagination. It means reading voices we've never heard before and stories from places we've never been.' The same goes for 2021.

You know a short story is good when it shoves you. Sometimes they're uncomfortable, funny, outrageous or strange; some provide escapism; others throw their troubles at you or even reveal your own. The best writers are able to rearrange the way you view the world sentence by sentence. I love the feeling of my brain readjusting to a new logic as a story progresses, my assumptions and understanding overturned by each word, and after the final line, that delicious moment when you're aware your brain's been subtly altered. George Saunders put it better in *A Swim in a Pond in the Rain*: 'that's what fiction does: it causes an incremental change in the state of a mind. That's it. But, you know – it really does it.

That change is finite but real.' He also says, and I agree, that writing's job is to 'wake us up'.

A usual way to wake up is to travel, but when we can't, we can read ourselves away. This anthology transports us to Berlin, London, Colombo, Kuala Lumpur, Jaffna, an Irish housing estate, a Cornish farming village, a Shabbat kitchen, Birmingham NEC, an island with a steep hill, and deep into the internet. You'll encounter a history of thievery, ambitious chicken consumption, foot and mouth, gender injustice, fleeting intimacy, poisonous fungi, alcoholism, a muscled film star, the South Circular, a starfish bride, extreme hunger and first kisses; be called a dumb-dumb; witness suicide, ghosting, drug dealers, parental angst, online creeps; meet village elders, go to the football, work out, make risotto, and attend school in Sri Lanka. All this can be experienced from your armchair, your bed or on a bus.

The longest story in this collection is just shy of 5,000 words, or about 20 pages; that's not long. Irenosen Okojie says of short fiction, 'There's no room for endless flourishes with language or space to leave threads you can take time coming back to. Every sentence has to earn its place.' In these twelve stories, every sentence does. Stories also need to feel fresh and original, according to John Cheever: 'One never puts down a sentence without the feeling that it has never been put down before in such a way.' The best fiction does this, and as a reader, you're left in the pleasurable wake of the writer's imagination. That's the kind of work we're looking for in this competition.

Each year I invite a writer, publisher and agent I admire to judge the prize. I saw Wendy Erskine read her story 'NOTES

FOR [. . .]' at a Brick Lane Bookshop event a few years ago, which inspired me to read her collection *Sweet Home*, and I promptly became a massive fan of her funny, dark and clever work.

I asked Kishani Widyaratna because her name was often mentioned in the acknowledgements of books I loved. While at Picador, she worked with Raven Leilani, Olivia Laing, Sarah Moss and many others. Now Editorial Director at 4th Estate, she is 'drawn to stories that illuminate the world we live in, writers who push boundaries and exceptional writing that cuts through everything'.

I met Elise Dillsworth at a London Short Story Prize event some years ago so I knew she liked short fiction. Elise has a background in publishing and set up her own literary agency in 2012. In 2020 she moved to David Higham Associates, where she represents many brilliant writers, including short-story great Irenosen Okojie.

All three judges were impressed by the quality, breadth and varied nature of the longlist but the only story they all totally agreed on was our 2021 winner, 'Earth-Grown Bodies', for its control, complexity and striking imagery. There was a jostle for the shortlist and it took some tense, thoughtful pauses and valiant compromises before the judges decided on our top six. I could not predict which would land on top, and Wendy said she could've been convinced any one of them was the standout.

Another aim of this competition is to give new writers confidence to continue writing, and to connect them to each other and to new readers. We can't take credit for previous longlistees' successes, but there have been many and we can watch in awe: Isha Karki has won multiple other competitions and is now judging the Galley Beggar Press Short Story Prize. Judith Wilson won the London Short Story Prize, Jack Houston was shortlisted for the BBC National Short Story Award, Rosanna Hildyard's 'Slaughter' was longlisted for the Edge Hill Short Story Prize, Melody Razak's debut novel *Moth* is a lead fiction title from Weidenfeld & Nicolson. Huma Qureshi's short-story collection *Things We Do Not Tell the People We Love* sold in a four-way auction and is out this November, Gemma Reeves' debut novel *Victoria Park* is a bestseller in Brick Lane Bookshop. Alice Haworth-Booth wrote *Protest! How people have come together to change the world*, and she and her sister Emily (who illustrated the book) painted our bookshop window to celebrate its publication day. I look forward to seeing what the 2021 longlistees do next. I have high hopes.

Being in the right space to write is tricky, especially when the news is distracting. You have to find that fragile balance between total concentration and complete mental freedom. These twelve writers managed it in another very strange year and I hope you enjoy their work as much as I do. Carmen Maria Machado says of her writing process: 'I just have to set myself up to be as open and responsive to stimuli as I possibly can be.' It's a decent aim, for writing and life.

Kate Ellis
Project Manager Brick Lane Bookshop Short Story Prize
September 2021

**Brick Lane Bookshop
Short Story Prize**
Longlist 2021

Earth-Grown Bodies

Aoife Inman

In the month before they begin burning animals on the Gower farm, there is a party in the village hall. It is organised by the Young Farmers' Club. There is a bar serving cans of Coke and 7UP and the committee repurpose the silver Christmas streamers they used during the infant nativity as decorations for the windows. By seven the hall is busy. The Gowers' eldest boy, Liam, hangs around the entranceway with James Trewin and Moira Lewis, slouching against the doorframe and blocking it just enough that people have to step over his feet. He kicks his younger brother, Dylan, in the shin as he passes and flicks a red plastic lighter with his thumb so that the flame dances on and off. Liam is taller than his peers, with pale, almost-white hair, shaved to the scalp. There is an inch-long scar on his ear lobe where Moira once pierced it with a safety pin and slipped. The three of them laugh disparagingly at the younger children darting back and forth from the dance floor, faces red with exertion, and at half past eleven they stalk off towards one of the old barns on the edge of the Gowers' land. They've bought pills from Dom Evans, hidden in a plastic tampon applicator in Moira's bag, though there is no one on the door of the village hall to search their things and the pretence feels childish now. They climb up onto the roof to take them. It's a full moon and the corrugated iron ripples like the surface of a lake. From a distance they can hear the music blaring from the hall. *Cotton-Eye Joe*. The sky is vast and black. Liam opens his mouth and imagines it pouring inside him like tar. A torch beam swings across the hill and at some point they climb down and head back to their respective houses, running blindly up the empty country roads, their pupils wide.

There is talk of what is coming long before it arrives and the village takes precautions. The Lewises leave buckets of bleach solution at the farm gate and the sound of hosepipes sluicing down cattle grids seems to last all day.

Gwennol Day comes and goes. The livestock shows are cancelled so the celebration feels smaller than usual without the Trewins' barns set out with rows of pens for all the rams and heifers. Still, the parade in the centre of the village goes ahead and the rain holds off.

A man from the council comes on a weekend and helps to close the footpaths that lead through the fields, until the valley is bisected in every direction by yellow tape.

This works for a while. Spring settles in as normal. Overnight, there are swallows nesting on the side of the schoolhouse and snowdrops appear on the verge by the newer housing estate at the base of the village. The ten o'clock news shows videos of fires on the Devon border. The cameras cut away to shots of empty yards and redundant milking equipment. Everybody in the village watches, switching channels when the news returns to the presenters in the studio, to catch the last few minutes of a programme about trains or weight loss on one of the satellite channels.

'It doesn't mean anything till it's here, just a lot of words to scare us,' Liam's mother, Roxanne, tells her sons, frying sausages on two flat griddle pans. Fat from the meat spits up onto her jumper, her forearms, her hair and she rubs it in with her damp fingers.

Liam shrugs his shoulders. 'You can't stir shit without a stick.'

'Language. Your brother's sat right there.' Roxanne looks over at her husband, Martin, slumped by the window overlooking the field. He massages the corner of his jaw with two fingers, frowning. He has been grinding his teeth in his sleep again. She calls his name and flicks her eyes towards their eldest son.

He sighs. 'Whatever you're doing, Liam, stop it.'

'Right, that'll be nothing, then. I'll stop doing nothing.'

Martin presses his wrists into the arms of his chair, exhales, and leaves the room. Roxanne hears the latch on the front door click to and she jostles the sausages in the pan so hard their skins split, juices hissing against the hot oil.

Roxanne Gower isn't a superstitious woman, but she isn't one to take chances either. There is a psychic from Trennelow Downs whose number Polly from the PTA meetings had slipped her last week.

'I can tell there's something on your mind,' Polly said across the table when they stopped for a smoke break. 'And she's not half-cut this one. It's the real deal. It was her that told me to get my thyroid checked last January, you remember?'

When the boys have left Roxanne rings her. The dialling tone goes on for a long time and the voice that answers the phone is low and hoarse. It has a smoker's crackle to it and

Roxanne hangs up before she can ask her name.

In March a calf is born on the Gower farm. Liam is driving round the slope of the back field when he spots the heifer lying flat on the grass. The calf comes out legs first, body lodged between the safety of its mother and the spring air.

'I don't blame you, my love,' Liam says when he climbs down. 'It's a right mess out here. Best to hang tight.'

He holds the stiff, still legs of the calf and strokes the stomach of its mother, taut and dark. The field is quiet. Reaching up inside the animal, he twists the thick fleshy band that has caught around the calf's neck. He feels it is dead before it concertinas out, slick with life, stiff with the lack of it. Waiting in the cold air, he calls Kathy Morley, although he knows there is nothing to be done. The mother hangs her head back against the ground for a moment, eyes silted, before getting up, walking off the loss.

'That there's a sign,' Roxanne Gower says when she comes down from the house with Liam's brothers, and, sure enough, it is. When Kathy arrives, there are blisters on the feet of half the herd, small enough to miss the first time around, but clear enough to see now.

Roxanne doesn't know quite what to do with the news so she invites the young woman inside the house. She makes a pot of tea, sets her youngest boy down in front of a video. She wonders where Martin is. She hasn't seen him since the morning. He'd been down on the east fields tedding grass for silage. The hum of the tractor had woken her and she'd looked over at the empty space in the sheets beside her, running her fingers over the dip in the mattress, noticing the hairs caught on the pillowcase.

It doesn't take long for news of the infection to spread. Vans and army transport trucks arrive on the farm, loaded with paper masks and polythene sheeting. They replace the troughs of household bleach solution at the entrances to the barns and fields with buckets of lye and stiff brushes. The air smells so clean there can be no doubt the land is sick.

As soon as the quarantine is placed on the Gowers' farm, James Trewin is seen taking one of his calves, a steer, down the cliff path to the bay. He has remembered a story he'd been told once as a child, about a ritual amongst sailors. They would carry an ailing man down to meet the incoming tide and when the water retreated, so would his fever. James bargains something like that will work as good for cows as it does for men, as a pre-emptive measure at least. He leaves early, dressed in a rugby jersey, jogging bottoms and flip-flops. He leads the animal out of the farm's western gate and round the headland. There is a thin path, worn into the heather of the cliffside, that curls steeply down towards the sand and he takes this, holding on to the rope around the calf's neck with one fist, coaxing it slowly down the hill.

Ruth Kessell is standing on the flat serpentine rock beds at the far side of the bay. Her son Isaac is collecting hermit crabs in a bucket by the edge of the water. She spots James and watches for a while. She is waiting on the tide too. Right now the beach is half its full length, but when the waves have waned, exposing the pale body of sand, she will head out to the surf rocks where mussels grow in thick bunches. Nobody bothers to collect them here anymore; most don't even know they grow on this coast.

When boy and calf arrive down on the sand, James slaps the skin behind the animal's shoulders, rubbing the clay-coloured hair into a cowlick, then brushing it flat with his fingers, the

5

way his mum had done with him when he was small. They walk to the shoreline, sinking ankle-deep into the silt.

The tide is going out. Ruth zips up her parka, calls out for Isaac, and makes her way through the tide pools to where the water cracks into foam over the green rock heads.

James leads the calf into the water. He slips his palm under the rope on the calf's neck and feels the warm heat of its body against his skin. He closes his eyes and imagines the infection running out of every orifice, clotting in the water like oil. When he looks up, the calf bends its neck to the water and sinks its nose in, dark eyes damp with salt. He stares at it for a while. Well, that'll be something, he thinks to himself, nodding.

Dripping, they turn and head back up the way they have come.

When the MAFF vans come to the Trewin farm the following day, James tells them they must have got something wrong.

'We've got no sick animals here. You want the Gowers' over the way.'

The man on the doorstep nods sympathetically. 'Is your dad around?'

'The Gowers' land is on quarantine – they've got cases up there, it was on the news.' James nods his chin towards the van on the driveway. 'Have you dipped the wheels on that? You shouldn't even be coming up here if you haven't.'

The man clears his throat. 'Listen, we called ahead, spoke to your dad. It's a pre-emptive measure,' he says. 'We're taking all the animals in a three-kilometre radius of the test site.'

James grips the doorframe with his fists. 'That's fucking illegal, that is. You can't take shit without a warrant. Come back with a warrant, yeah?'

Harvey Trewin appears in the hallway behind James and places a hand on his shoulder, squeezing softly. 'It's all right now. Let him in.'

Harvey is a soft-spoken man, which has never mattered much to James until now. He shrugs off his dad's palm and curls his face into an expression of disgust, wiping the hair from his forehead with his fingers.

'You bastard,' he mutters, loud enough to hurt, and disappears out into the yard.

When it starts, Martin Gower insists on helping to bring the animals up the field, although Roxanne tries to persuade him otherwise.

'You'll only make a mess of yourself. No need to put yourself through all that. Let them do their job.'

'They're my animals,' he says. 'My responsibility what happens to them.'

'I'll help,' Liam says, leaning through the kitchen door on his way upstairs.

'You'll do no such bloody thing,' Roxanne hisses.

'He's man enough now,' Martin says calmly. 'If he wants to.'

'I'm his mother. I'll say when he's a man and it isn't now.'

'I'm not going to sit in the house while it's happening.'

'You'll do what you're told.' Roxanne spins round to face her son.

'Let him help. It's the best thing. Got to learn to deal with all things on a farm, death included. That's just the way of it.'

'This isn't death, Martin. It's the whole bleddy farm. You want him to watch that all be taken?' Roxanne cries then, ugly sobbing, wiping down her cheeks with the back of her hand. 'You selfish bastard.' The men in the room – because they are now, both of them, men – look away, fidget with their hands a little, picking the dirt under their nails. Martin Gower mutters his wife's name quietly under his breath, pleading something, although the request never quite falls out straight and they exchange a cold stare.

'Well, I want to help,' Liam says, unfolding his arms and helping himself to a slice of toast from the table.

Roxanne turns away towards the hob and takes a boiling pan off the heat, using a slotted spoon to remove the eggs, the steam condensing on their shells like a second skin. 'You don't know what you want,' she says softly, tipping the eggs into a bowl in the centre of the table, before leaving the room. It is important, she thinks, to have the last word, even if it means nothing at all.

The following day they begin burning livestock on the Gower farm. The parish newsletter announces the time and date of the fires on its back page beneath the obituaries, although it's clear from the sound what is happening. They build the pyres on the top field, the bodies of the animals partially obscured by an outbuilding. Six hundred Holstein Friesians. On the road that leads up towards the farm, the gate is drawn across and men in white coveralls are seen on the bridleway, moving the last of the cattle from the Lewis and Trewin farms up the track and spraying down their vehicle tyres with bleach.

The smoke begins in the evening. Isaac Kessell leaves his bedroom blind open and presses his forehead against the

8

windowpane.

'Jonah's dad is taking him up to watch from the field,' he tells his mum, eyes fixed on the road outside. 'Everybody'll be there.'

'It's a school night,' Ruth says, rubbing her thumb over a grease stain on her son's blue football shirt. 'Why d'you want to go watch that anyway?'

Isaac wriggles his shoulders out from her grasp. 'Jonah said, last year, Martin Gower put a fridge in the bonfire on the hill and when it caught light it exploded. That's why he's got that funny scar on his eyebrow. It got all singed off with the sparks.'

Ruth presses her lips together, trying not to smile.

'Well, it's cows they've got on those fires, not fridges.'

'I know that.' Isaac rolls his eyes.

There's a small moon-shaped night light in the corner of the room, which Ruth switches on. It casts a faint yellow glow across the carpet. Isaac can't sleep without it, even though he's nine. Ruth has tried removing it and stowing it in a drawer in the kitchen, but he finds and puts it back every time. She frowns as she watches him climb into the bed, his feet, pale as minnows, slipping out from beneath the covers.

'Do you think he's too sensitive, the way he is?' she'd asked her mum the previous day as they took Isaac for a walk down the woods where the crocus bulbs were coming through. Isaac had been showing them how to spot vole holes in the dry-stone walling that ran along the edge of the path, digging his fingers into the tussock grass and revealing opening after opening, each one dark brown, damp, and as delicate as an egg.

'He'll toughen up,' her mum had replied. 'And then

9

you'll wish he hadn't – I remember when your brother asked for a Swiss Army knife for Christmas, I near on cried.'

Isaac's small body softens as he drifts to sleep, knees tucked to his chest, and Ruth sighs. She walks downstairs, runs the water hot to soak the chicken pan and opens the back door. The daylight has stretched a half-hour thinner than the previous evening and the air is murky and rust-coloured, illuminating the quiet farm and smog gathering on the hill.

Later, Liam drives around the fields with his father. They don't talk. They have never been good at that sort of thing. Martin Gower lets his son take the wheel as they loop to the south fields, their backs to the pyres at the top of the hill. Once, when Liam was small, he took his son around this very route. 'One day, this'll be yours, eh now? What about that?' he'd said aloud, one broad palm clasping Liam's tiny chest to his own.

Now, he leaves Liam to drive the rest of the route alone, checking for any calves that are left, that have managed to squeeze past the old fence posts and down to the river. Martin stands and watches his son, one hand on the wheel, the other hanging languidly at his hip, as the tractor bounces up the curl of the hill and out of sight.

The weather over the weekend is damp and changeable, and the fires have to be reset several times as new banks of cloud roll over the hills. It's the fine sort of rain, the kind that hangs threadlike, suspended rather than settling, and it can't clear the smoke from the air. The smell of the burning animals lingers, a noose around the B-road that leads down into the village.

In the evening, on the television, they show footage of

the fires and Ruth lets Isaac stay up to watch. He's wearing Batman pyjamas and the elastic around the cuffs is thin and loose from where his limbs have grown too quickly. When the camera pans out to show the pyres at the top of the hill behind their house, Isaac leans forward on his knees and points out the navy hoodies and trainers of his school friends at the edge of the frame.

'If you'd let me go, I'd have been on telly too,' he says. 'Then Auntie Sue could have watched.'

Ruth mutes the broadcaster, who is repeating the same well-worn statistics about infection rates that they've been hearing for weeks. She accepts an orange segment from her son and they watch the screen as a blue lorry with an open storage bed empties carcasses onto the grass, their thick bodies crumpling into one another like paint squeezed from a tube. Martin Gower is standing in the foreground, behind the correspondent with his clean wax jacket. His face is gaunt, the burst capillaries on his cheekbones bright under the camera lights. Isaac drops the orange peel onto the coffee table and climbs onto the sofa, sliding his head under the crook of Ruth's arm.

'Will they get more animals now, new ones?' he asks.

'I expect so, yeah. They'll have to, else it won't be a farm, not really.'

Isaac screws his face into a knot. 'How do they kill them?' he asks.

'The vet shoots them in the head – that's what's kindest.'

He hugs her then and Ruth wonders if this is too much detail for a nine-year-old.

Ten days after the ashes are buried, the quarantines on the

11

farms are lifted and one by one the MAFF vans leave the village, but the acrid smell of the fires lingers. Liam, James and Moira are seen at the White Lion. The barman, George, knows their parents, their farms. He serves them halves of pale ale, which they take to the corner and drink quickly, in silence. A small group sets up the pool table in the back of the pub and the gentle click of cues echoes across the bar.

Moira unrolls a packet of gum on the table.

'Dad heard from Harry Pope that they think it was some cows up at Holsworthy Market that brought it down this way.' She flicks her gaze between the boys' faces, then shrugs and slips a piece of gum between her teeth. 'I don't know, you know, but that's what people are saying.'

James picks the edges of a beer mat. 'Your dad buys from Holsworthy, doesn't he, Liam?'

Liam spits into his empty glass. 'Whole bloody county goes there, dickhead.'

'I'm just saying . . .' James shrugs.

It's Liam who swings first. Something smashes, cracks, and people turn expecting broken glass and the sticky residue of spirits. The boys are not really fighters but they make a good go of it. They throw their bodies at one another and push their fists and teeth into the skin of shoulders and cheeks. Moira flattens her back against the panelled wall of the alcove and the boys slam one another onto the dirty carpet in front of the bar. The pool cues at the back of the pub are leant against the table, and George drags the boys out into the street, one under each arm.

'That'll do,' he says, wiping his palms against his thighs and picking up the bottles that have been left on the doorstep by the early-evening drinkers. 'I think we've seen enough of all that. Piss off before I ring your dad, Liam.'

The boys spit on the tarmac and walk off. Whatever has been said in those punches feels beyond repair.

That summer is cooler than the previous year but people still come down for the holidays. Ruth Kessell drives over to the rental cottages by the bay in early July and goes around opening the upstairs windows. She bleaches the sinks and the showers and lays out fresh towels in the bedrooms. The bookings on the website are full until September. People seem to have forgotten about the images of vets in paper coveralls patrolling the countryside. Good, Ruth thinks, the sooner the better.

A family from York arrive midweek and park up on the verge. Ruth recognises them. They come most years at the same time, like clockwork. A mother, a father, two young children, a boy and a girl.

'Your husband took them to feed the calves up at the farm last time we were here. They loved that,' the mother tells Ruth animatedly when she drops round the following week to replace a bulb in the kitchen. 'Is he around?' she asks.

'Nah, not anymore.'

'Sometimes they're more trouble than they're worth.' The woman laughs lightly and touches her hand to her mouth. Behind her, the man is teaching his daughter how to shuffle a pack of cards. Ruth smiles and asks if they have enough loo roll in the bathrooms.

'We saw the news, you know . . .' The man is standing now, one hand around his wife's shoulders, thumb to her collarbone. 'About the farms,' he continues, 'but we didn't know if it was here . . . whether they would have had to . . .'

13

Ruth nods and the woman frowns, chewing her lip. 'Oh that's awful, just horrible to think about.'

'Yeah.' There is a small silence. Ruth wipes her hands on her jeans. 'That's all done for you now so I'll be off.'

'Oh right, thanks, that's great.' The woman slips a hand into her pocket and pulls out a fiver.

'You're all right.' Ruth shakes her head. 'It's just a bulb.'

'No please, you went to all that trouble.'

Ruth's cheeks feel hot but she pockets the note and slips out onto the road. She spots Liam Gower in the village-hall car park at the base of the hill. His bike is leant against the low wall and he is rolling a cigarette with his back to the sea.

'You all right?' she calls.

He nods.

'Need a lift home? You can chuck the bike in the back if you want.'

'Nah, I'm grand.' He gives her a half smile and cups his hand around the lighter, chewing smoke into the air. Moira Lewis comes out from behind the hall itself and shifts her eyes about from Liam to Ruth.

'All right, Mrs Kessell,' she says, biting her nail. 'How's Isaac?'

'He's good, thanks for asking. You lot off for summer now?'

'Something like that, yeah.'

'How's your folks holding up?'

Ruth has seen Martin Gower round and about. He looks old now, and worried. She knows money is tight. Compensation is meant to be coming but there are still infected sites up around the Welsh border, Yorkshire, Dartmoor. Everything has ground to a standstill.

The two of them shrug. 'You know,' they say. 'It's all . . .' and they tail off.

'Yeah,' Ruth says, nodding. 'Been a bit like that.'

On the farm, Roxanne Gower wakes up next to her husband for the first time in years. The air is hot in the small room and she moves the covers from her legs, aware of the damp warmth that has greased itself around her ankles and toes. She lies there as the sun creeps across the duvet, scattering fragments of warm summer light along the opposite wall.

Martin is awake too. Roxanne can feel the slackness of his breathing against her arm, his spine turned towards her. She pretends to fall asleep again, and when she opens her eyes he is gone. The back door scuffs. She hears his footsteps on the gravel drive and she exhales. Her children are waking up. The toaster pops. The smell of lemon shower gel and steam from the bathroom seeps across the landing; the window has been left shut again even though she tells them every day it will rot the woodwork. Her younger boys are arguing over the television remote. She closes her eyes and tries to remember what it was like before she was married but it is so long ago now that the memories are dull, their surface scummed over by age and tax bills.

The day of the rescheduled school exams is warm, too warm, and the teaching assistant, Cathi, opens the row of windows in the eaves of the school hall to let in a small breeze. Only Moira and James turn up. Moira lingers in the entranceway, wrapping a hair elastic around her wrist and snapping it against her skin, but eventually she slides into her seat. Cathi keeps the door open a few minutes longer than she should. She is hoping Liam will saunter in, trainer laces trailing along the corridor, but he doesn't.

'Miss, it's nine, can we turn these over now?' James chews the end of his pen and tries to read the questions through the back of the paper. Someone has written the sine formula in blue biro on the desk he is sitting at and he holds his finger over it, feeling the little ridges in the wood.

Cathi exhales, frowns, shuts the door. 'Let's go, then. Forty minutes, you know the drill.' She walks back towards the stage, pausing to pick up the spare answer paper from the desk near the front.

A group of walkers come to stay at the holiday lets over the bank holiday weekend. The footpaths around the village have been reopened but they are quieter than usual, even on the popular routes. James Trewin finds two of them out by the lower fields, climbing over a stile that used to lead around the peninsula to the smaller cove, a half-mile along the cliffs.

'Have you dipped those?' He nods to their boots, caked in river mud and gravel dust.

They smile and rub the insect bites on their lower arms. 'Sorry, mate. We didn't know.'

There is a bucket of bleach and water, along with a brush, stacked against the metal livestock gate. James sucks in his cheeks and a muscle in his jaw flexes.

'There's a sign up,' he says. 'Might be right of way, but don't be a prick about it.'

The taller of the two men holds his hands up. 'Honest mistake,' he calls. 'You have a good day.' He turns back towards the stile and James shakes his head. 'Wanker,' he mutters and clicks his tongue.

The summer turns over and the schools go back. The roads are quieter. There are crab apples on the ground by the wall of the church, their skins wrinkled and reddy-brown.

Liam Gower is seen up at the old bird-watching hut with Moira Lewis. Nobody says anything to their parents. Some things are best kept quiet – this is the general consensus.

The post office closes down. A fundraiser is held to keep a volunteer there one day a week – cake sales, a tombola, guess the name of the bear – but it turns up short and they have to shut anyway.

Ruth drives down to the holiday lets and strips the beds, airing the mattresses and wiping down the skirting boards. There are two bookings for October, one for New Year's – plenty of time to prepare.

Just before the first cold spell begins, Martin Gower's body is found slung up in the copse of trees near the church. Roxanne senses something is wrong from the hum of the village when she wakes. The earth outside is quiet. Downstairs the boiler moans and she hears the taps going in the kitchen. The bedroom window is open a crack and the siren whistles up the lane, quietens, parks, pauses. She rolls over and slides her feet out to fill the space on the far side of the bed, waiting for the knock at the door.

WATCH AND SUBSCRIBE!!
Artemisia eats entire Chicken Shop Menu – Mukbang LIVE!

Danielle Vrublevskis

takes me an hour to prep (wifi, angles, make-up, lighting)

I get the bags of food ready and visible on the desk, waiting like bombs, and I open the first one and take out onion rings, hold them up to the camera, and then begin

I'm chewing before I even start to stream

got the jump on all the viewers as they log on, loyal as praetorians, to watch me eat

wings, thighs, breast, got chips delivered too and even the flaccid salad and I say this last one aloud and get

17:00 [no profile pic]: >:(

17:00 [no profile pic]: porn
gif, the woman's eyes
sometimes shown

but my eyes twinkle as I eat, I have special contact lenses that make them brighter and bluer – anime beauties, Superman X-ray, Merlin who could see into the future

today I'm eating the entire chicken shop menu – Kent Fried Chicken, the copyright-avoiding colonel with a brown beard instead of a white one

I went there once after a night out and a man said to me cheesy chips were a girly order when all around us was lovely meat, cut and portioned right to fit in greasy little boxes

> 17:05 [no profile pic]: Flat 7
> Naples Road, Islington,
> N1–

17:05: deleted

17:05: sorry babes that's private, wink gif, haha

> 17:06 [profile pic him in
> graduate gown]: that her
> address?

it's wrong anyway, idiots think I'm still at my old place but now if anybody went there they'd find only a baffled bougie couple and an underexercised greyhound

> 17:07 [the graduate gown
> accented by fur]: she's
> not interested in you
> losers

salad is too warm, chicken is too cold, its skin pimpled, my skin pimpled too from wearing only a strappy top, the kind that mothers in films would look at and say you're not going out in that but I wasn't going out

I wasn't going anywhere because my hour of streaming today would keep me for the week

wool scratches below my waist from the blanket that none of my viewers can see

> 17:13 [profile pic a cartoon
> girl]: feet pics?

I send him my business email address, those cost more and only when I am in the mood – £100 per foot, my little toes expensive as saffron, more reliable than gold

my face, back at me, deliberately pretty

my room, behind me, discarded PhD drafts, sheaves of paper stuffed into bookshelves, laundry whirring through a cycle downstairs, shuddering my feet, maybe I put a red in with that white wash, I can't remember and can't check now

they like a messy room, makes me human, though they don't know how I watch them back

they aren't aware of the hours I spend on my academic research combing through chatrooms:

skinny boys with painted-on abs

women pointing to the bags under their eyes and asking whether they are hideous

flesh edited out of existence by filters, girls becoming hourglasses, men turning triangular

oh, they are all a little lovely, my audience, all have beauty in them

> 17:22 [profile pic a little girl]: fatty
>
> 17:25 [profile pic a ninja]: I want to turn you inside out

17:25: blocked

> 17:25 [profile pic a fitness model]: he was complimenting you

conference days I speak about all this online chatter in rooms that smell of coffee and sweat and all these scholars look at me and wait for what insights will come out of my mouth next

I once overheard this professor say she was working

21

class because she sold her ideas and wasn't that comparable to retail/factory/delivery drivers/cleaners?

now into the burger and chips, classic as a nuclear family

grease drops and hits my blanket

it'll smell of burgers for the rest of the week, even after I've aired out the room and lit some incense, vanilla? cinnamon? no it's a lavender sort of week after this, for rest and forgetting and sweetness

there were lavender sprigs under my pillow every night when that deepfake video first came out and I couldn't sleep without thinking of all the angles from which I could be seen (couldn't be seen – that version wasn't me and yet it had my eyes, sometimes, because they'd sourced my face from my hundreds of streams, accurately, carefully)

I wonder sometimes about the body they stitched me onto, who she was, whether she knew that they'd taken her head, whether she cared

sometimes I dream I meet her

we hug, finally complete

we turn into something incredible, a robot, a unicorn, something more than the sum of our parts, but I still never see her face

no time to dream, I keep going with the chips, sprinkling vinegar onto them, so strong it pouts my mouth

> 17:31 [profile pic a fitness model]: rub it on your tits, £10

17:32: not that kind of channel babe x

> 17:32 [profile pic a fitness model]: fucking right it's not

they sign off, another viewer lost but one in 10,000, as statistically significant as the odds of being injured by a toilet or winning an Oscar and I don't worry about those

the Academy is still yet to contact me of course

I smile, and my viewers think it's for them

> 17:37 [no profile pic]: it's all fake
>
> 17:39 [no profile pic]: making me feel less lonely this evening, thank you xxxxxoxox £50

17:40: thanxxx love u guys

> 17:41 [profile pic a bear]: too skinny
>
> 17:41 [the bear is fighting]: vomiting gif 1
>
> 17:41 [profile pic an actual bear-baiting screenshot]: bet she throws it up afterwards

wrong

there's a wilderness survival programme I watch where the women always do better than the men, and this woman kills a squirrel and as its flayed skin is steaming heat into her eyes she looks up to heaven and then to the ground and says thanks, like that squirrel was put in that forest just for her

so I have never thrown up any of the food I eat for these videos because there was a potato once in the dark warmth of the soil that was destined for this: for picking and chopping and freezing and frying, and that unsuspecting potato is now covered in ketchup and glory as I stream it to thousands of followers there's a reason for everything, I've heard many times, said to me like an apology

the vibration on my feet changes from heavy bass to whining melody and on to a final spin, can't leave the clothes in there too long or my room-mate will leave a passive-aggressive note full of :) and ! and ?

it's not me in the deepfake but technology can do some marvellous things and stitch a girl's face onto another girl's body so neatly that nobody can tell the difference, and that was three years ago so imagine what they could do now, have probably already done

I still don't know who made it, no way of finding out the police said, and not a crime anyway so why bother them, don't I know there are proper villains out there not some little weirdo I should pity, maybe even forgive?

> 17:49 [profile pic a Kardashian]: she's got a filter on

no filter right now, and I'm on to the ice cream which is so sweet I taste only pink not strawberries (strawberry flavour says the packet defensively)

I frown when I bite into it and feel the cold bloom up my teeth and you can't fake that and this is mine, all the tips I get, an honest living

> 17:51 [profile pic a white man in a suit, it's his real picture and he should be careful talking to strangers on the internet, a man like that could be taken advantage of]: £176

apart from the 15% platform fee

there have to be ways to diversify

17:55: I'm thinking of moving into ASMR x

                17:55 [no profile pic]: so cool!

                17:55 [profile pic a famous
                          blonde singer]: yesss

                17:55 [profile pic maybe not
                          that blonde singer,
                          maybe a famous female
                          fascist]: porn gif, no
                          eyes shown

an email is sent to my work from a burner account every year or so, titled: *re inappropriate video*

the department are kinder than they need to be about the deepfake, and offer counselling each time (as if I don't already do it), though they think thank God not my daughter/wife/ girlfriend but I bet some of them don't even know, haven't checked how somebody can turn an image sour

I sometimes think about finding out who did it, stitching their head into some awful video but that would be lowering myself to revenge and that never works out in the films though it looks such fun

my outfit for misguided, hollow, entertaining revenge: trousers (leather), blouse (red), gloves (many pairs for different crimes)

the ice cream is done now on to the showstopper the finale

                17:57 [profile pic definitely
                        a famous blonde
                        fascist]: she's not going
                        to manage that whole
                        chicken now

I'm going to more than manage it, I'm going to develop

it like an underperforming employee, I'm going to give it a performance review and team-building days

it's the size of my head but I've always liked a challenge and I eat it methodically from the bottom up like bears do to unfortunate hikers and I pause when I can and tell the viewers to follow, to like and subscribe and pay and they do and I see my heating bill, a good night out, a new laptop and still the money keeps rising and still I keep eating

my stomach doesn't hurt at all though it should, my insides are resilient

fingers have wrinkled from the grease and my palms smell of fat

mascara has run a little

> 18:01 [no profile pic]: hot
> 18:01 [profile pic a selfie of a boy not even old enough for the platform and he's got a little dog in his arms]: £4.50

a jingle from below and my wash is done and the chicken is done too and what a well-planned day

I log off and I collect my laundry – the room-mate has put her next load on top of the machine to mark her spot in the queue but she's out now at her 9to5

I put my blanket in next for a whole three-hour cycle and look at cottage getaways for next weekend while I wait

Reputation Management

Katherine Gutierrez

The woman has a job as a professional liar. Her lies aren't long and they aren't meant to be. They appear to thousands of people across the world, sometimes in Malay, sometimes English. Her lies are ideally three lines long, inane, unaffected by the most recent MAS union strike, divorces, the shattering realities of the DMV. She's meant to sell a corner. The corner is half hope, half home improvement.

> *The Redux hairdryer is better than I thought! The four power settings really help control how much heat you use on your hair. My hair is very fine and sensitive, so I am pleased with this purchase! Recommend!!*

She will then refine, rephrase, repost. Facebook, Mudah, Shopee and Reddit, interspersing among her fifty to eighty accounts, marking off days and sites on her desk calendar with different coloured pens. Suspicious if a windfall of five-star and four-star reviews suddenly hits the net. People like her have been outed before, a collage of all their posts gathered into one large callout post accompanied by an essay on consumerism and morality. These callout posts are given thousands of upvotes. Her job requires a certain indifference to society and a peeling away from the unspoken code of the little people versus the big corporations. Not that she has many friends anyway.

Every day she looks for new opportunities and stares for hours at her phone screen. Outside, the threat level is amber and the bug-shaped zebra doves on the dentist's veranda are gone. All the avifauna of Kuala Lumpur are waiting out this latest typhoon in their ancestral hideaways.

Her apartment is on the eleventh and highest floor, the building itself blocked from eastern and western light by the merbau that were planted there years before. The merbau have grown well as they are on lowland and they are ten minutes from the banks of the Gombak. White flowers and seed pods are scattered on every surface, stuck into the crevices of windows and the hands of statues. The smell is loamy and slick. The smell for her is the smell of the city itself. When she is writing home to her mother she writes about the smell. The smell of her mother's house is cornstarch and laundry. Her mother's house is still boarded with corrugated iron and chicken wire, the stilts buckling with neglect.

The woman doesn't feel bad for the people who buy products at her false recommendation because they have money to spare. She and her mother never had anything to spare. The Redux hairdryer is RM1,500 and she rationalises that anyone who is willing to spend that amount of money on four different kinds of warm air should really be shot for the good of society.

Her clients are usually start-up businesses shilling services. Massage therapy, seaweed facial treatments, IUI and roofing. Some don't pay her in money but in vouchers, or they send gifts to her box in the mailroom. She has received American magazines, silk pillowcases, calendars and fabric purses containing rosaries. The rosaries are made of plastic and sometimes the saint is faceless, sometimes he is painted and bloody. She hangs all the rosaries she receives on her indoor banana fern along with a small portrait of solemn St Anthony, the saint of lost things, patron of the missing. She isn't Christian, the rosaries are gifts from her client in Chow Kit, but she thinks the trinkets of Christianity are pretty. All those royal blues and faces made of gold and pearl.

> *Thank you for my new face, Dr Arinzola! I was unsure at first. Like everyone else, I had seen the story of that girl featured on* The Fresh Eye, *but the price was just too reasonable to pass up! Facilities are very clean and the staff are very professional. Dr A was very calming and took great care of me and now I have the face I always wanted and am looking forward to applying for new job opportunities.*
>
> *Edit: For those asking, I had a rhinoplasty with malar implants!*
>
> *Second edit: And NO, I am not being paid to say these things! I genuinely had a wonderful experience. Bless.*

The woman's mother wrote to tell her that Nona will not walk the hour to school anymore. There have been rapes on the highway, two girls are still missing and they are no longer serving arepas before class so what was the point of wearing out the rubber on Nona's shoes?

The woman wrote back to ask if Nona wanted her to send books. What did she read now? It has been three years since her last visit and children's tastes change quickly. No more scratch and sniff or pull and listen to the farmyard animals. Princesses were probably the new flavour of the month. Didn't every little girl want to be a princess? The woman only remembers wanting to be a fish and swim lengths above a black ocean floor. She's still a good swimmer, even though she hasn't gone swimming in years. At least, she can remember how not to drown, which is the same thing.

Every morning the woman makes sure to move her muscles properly by lying on her back and following the simple rules of exertion, as shown to her in her YouTube exercise playlist. Eccentric, concentric, eccentric, concentric. She then makes tea, selecting from one of the many boxes of BOH that her client, who runs a laundromat, has sent her. Earl Grey with tangerine is her favourite.

The typhoon, rattling, shaking, making a maelstrom out of wind chimes and garden equipment, is like a friend speaking to her, sometimes dull and sometimes ranting. The threat alert is still amber, but she doesn't feel threatened at all.

By answering her emails she learns that her clients don't care about the typhoon either. In fact, a few of them have recognised the potential for profit. Gold Standard Movers see this as an opportunity to entice yacht owners with a once-in-a-decade deal to pull their moored yachts from the east peninsular. Lots of white people have their own holiday homes in Langkawi, but are currently in Houston, Cambridge, Moscow and will pay the exorbitant prices that Gold Standard have updated their website with.

She writes some reviews for their Google feed, praising their efficiency and skill in yacht-moving, designs a glowing Facebook post which she sends to them with her usual Photoshopped watermark and logs onto their CMS to help their developer, Ibrahim, change the front page. An hour later, she receives RM800 to her Paypal.

> *Was so happy to hear that GSM are now offering a Port Rescue service. My wife and I live in London and were worried about Storm Una sweeping our family yacht out to sea! We gave Adam the code to our mooring station and they can definitely be trusted. Adam and Yusuf were particularly helpful during this same-day process.*

The woman goes to the mailroom in her water shoes to collect a damp box containing Kenco coffee, socks from H&M and a small Chinese statue. This time, it's a lucky cat. Last time, it was a rooster. Honestly, she knows nothing about feng shui and keeps her statues next to her tree of saints. This box is from the massage parlour.

When she returns, she sees a new email in her inbox from an address she doesn't recognise. The email is from someone who had her services recommended to them by a fellow business in Brickfields, and now they want to know her rates and a list of success stories, times where she actively raised conversion, if such a document exists. They've included a link at the bottom of their email and she clicks it, thinking about how to explain to them that there was no discernible correlation between her false reviews and good business, especially if that business is already booming. More than likely, she calmed the fears of existing clients, people who were already planning to use the service and maybe, sometimes, attracted new clientele. It was reputation management rather than reputation elevation.

The link goes to a new-looking website with some fancy navigation and a silvery shoal of fish that shimmy to wherever the mouse arrow drifts. It is a restaurant's website, headed with the words 'The Smiling Fish'. The background is too heavy, an artistic depiction of incoming waves, the water realised with hard black lines and the fish as finger smudges. You can hardly read the catches of the day. This would be something to mention in her email back.

Her finger stills as she scrolls to the bottom of the page, to the slightly pixelated picture of 'the team' as they repeat the words 'family-owned' and 'shared dream' over and over.

The person in the middle of the picture is the Starfish Bride.

She would know the Starfish Bride anywhere, in any life. Upon occasion, the Starfish Bride still haunts the part of her brain that keeps a rich harvest of all the worst things she has done and all the terrible things she thinks about herself.

Before she made up lies for a paycheque and lived in a sky-level apartment near the river, she was living in an even more lively and expensive area near the National Museum. Even though she was elbow to elbow with beautiful sights, the botanical garden and the five-star hotels where lines of hospitality staff stood to attention for arriving limos and Mercedes-Benzes, she existed like a serf as an assistant shopkeep at Celestial Diamond.

Celestial Diamond was a bridal shop that catered to the wealthy from every background. The dresses, hairpieces, wigs and shoes were all overpriced, imported from East Asian factories. They catered to Muslim brides and Christian brides; they sold brocade Bhaku dress for Buddhist ceremonies.

The shop had some spare rooms on the lower floor. The largest was for storage (and the only lower room with air conditioning), another was for cleaning supplies, another stored electrical equipment and also had a mini kitchen where you could prepare tea and snacks for customers, another was a rickety WC with a glazed window that offered a glazed view of the gutters which often flooded with brown water, and the last room, the smallest one, was the one the woman was given as lodgings. For these lodgings, she surrendered most of her pay. The advertisement had said lodgings plus breakfast, but what was meant by breakfast was one bag of tea from the selection basket, as they kept the snack cupboards locked.

Celestial Diamond was run by two sisters and their mother: snobs who were paranoid about the next recession, sick at the mention of wealth distribution.

When the woman accepted the job, she quickly learnt that she was the only one working with them who was not a family member. Sometimes, even their twelve-year-old cousin would come in and help clean or sit by the mother to pin fabric as she made simple alterations to wedding dresses.

The woman had a strange fondness for the sisters, although she thought they were often ridiculous with embarrassing, fake charm. There was something vulnerable about them. They were like little girls in high heels.

The elder sister, Mahiran, was tall with big eyes that were

33

dark brown and often filled with tears. She wore designer clothes, shoes and bags that were all imported knock-offs. At a distance, she could be mistaken for a terribly elegant lady with her hair in a stewardess's chignon. Up close, you could see where her lipstick had smudged onto her chin, the soup stains on the cuffs of her fake Louis Vuitton blazer; she would be crying about something.

Her younger sister, Maziah, was a chameleon woman. One day she would be feet-up in the storage room reading magazines and smoking her e-cigarette, the next day she would be in her Friday best with her grandmother, denouncing the evils of the flesh. When she talked to older clients, she pretended that she had a two-year-old son, that her husband was a commercial pilot. She told this story so often and with so much confidence, so many interesting details, that it had become accepted among those who knew it wasn't true as simply an additional branch of her life, as if she existed in two different dimensions. So palpable was the tale that sometimes she would bring up her fake husband or fake son in conversation with her sister or mother, referring to them by the names she had made up, using them to win an argument.

When she met the Starfish Bride, the woman had worked there, on reception, making tea and arranging biscuits, organising the overfilled stockroom, for about a year. She had planned to stay longer. This had been when she was just out of night school, after leaving her job at Starbucks. She wasn't cut out for anything better, not yet.

The Starfish Bride had come in for several shopping sprees. She brought in an Oscar de la Renta wedding dress along with a laminated card that detailed alterations. She stood in front of the ceiling-to-floor mirror with her mother, sisters, brother-in-law's wife and a tiny, birdlike woman who was the wedding planner, and sampled every piece of jewellery, every shoe. Her party went through cups of tea and soda like a small army. The entire showroom appeared as though it had been overturned in a storm, all the opulent clutter, glitter and faux diamond, leading to the sacred, cleared circle in front of the mirror where the Starfish Bride stood like a queen.

Although Maziah commented that the Starfish Bride would need all that finery to distract from her dog face and Mahiran stress-cried at the aftermath of every visit, the sisters welcomed the Starfish Bride and her party because they were in awe of her. The Starfish Bride, who didn't, in fact, have a dog face, was educated, engaged to a wealthy man, and resistant to shame – all of the things the Celestial Diamond sisters longed to be.

The woman, the professional liar, had no strong feelings about the Starfish Bride. She even looked forward to each appearance because it broke up the monotony of the day. The Starfish Bride would always call the front desk an hour before arrival to make sure they could prepare adequately for her visit, which is something the woman wished all customers would do.

One day, the Starfish Bride dropped an email to the business inbox, sent by proxy of her wedding planner, to ask if anyone at Celestial Diamond knew of a vendor that would supply live produce for a wedding. Thinking she meant lobsters, Maziah emailed back to say they knew of a market that was close to the venue and could put in a call.

'What she expects from us, I don't know,' Maziah said. 'We're the dress shop, not the fucking caterers.'

The wedding planner, in a green coat that was so

oversized it made her look like a chess piece, arrived to give the sisters a small plastic box in which shells and sea crystal had been wrapped in a tea cloth.

'What can you do with this?' asked the wedding planner. 'Could you sew it into the dress?'

Mahiran looked scandalised. 'Into the de la Renta?'

'I need to call Mom.' Maziah pushed past her sister to find her iPhone in the storage room.

'The bride wants them deftly added. No hot glue. She wants them threaded in.'

The mother arrived and together, as a foursome, they stood over the plastic alteration table to pore through the box, each with a face of stone. The woman watched them with interest, but couldn't have guessed what was to come.

The Starfish Bride, it came to be known, had had a dream where her wedding took place underwater. The exact details were fuzzy, as the story took shape in snatches from the mother, Maziah and the wedding planner, but apparently sea gods and goddesses had attended in long gold robes, dolphins had pulled the Starfish Bride's wedding carriage; there had been candles floating in the water, lit with green flame.

'She's gone crazy,' Mahiran said. 'She's turned psychotic.'

'Let's get her to pay the rest of the money for the shoes and alterations now,' Maziah said. 'She still owes 30 per cent.'

The Starfish Bride had called that day, not for lobsters, but for starfish.

Her vision was to have live starfish at the ceremony and reception. She wanted them laid on tables, stuck to the walls of her ivory gazebo. She wanted starfish placed in blue silk that the children could carry instead of flowers. She wanted starfish to stick small parchment notes on that the bride and groom would write for each other.

The great flaw of this vision, of course, was that not one starfish would survive the event; each would suffocate within minutes once taken from the water. No one knew what a dead starfish at a wedding symbolised, but it seemed like a bad omen.

No one was able to convey this rationale to the Starfish Bride. She wouldn't even hear of having each starfish placed in a plastic bag filled with seawater; she definitely wouldn't hear of fake starfish made with acrylic and quartz.

'Surely this is a huge case for animal rights,' Maziah said. 'I know a few papers that would be all over this. I'm sure the nightly news would want to know about this mass starfish genocide.'

'What if we're implicated?' Mahiran whispered, her glossed lips wobbling. 'What if people boycott us with signs?'

'All publicity is good publicity,' Maziah said.

Grooms were a rare sight and the groom of the Starfish Bride was no exception. On the two occasions he had been to Celestial Diamond, everyone had agreed that he was too fine, that he looked like a darker Nicholas Teo.

The groom of the Starfish Bride had been sent to Celestial Diamond one evening with an updated list of corrections to the shoes and hairpieces. The woman was the only one at the front desk to greet him. The groom stayed, one arm crooked against the wall, and relayed all his apologies and concerns. '"Azure jackets," she says.' The groom gesticulated wildly. '"Tell me, honey, what is azure?" I say. You know, I would get married tomorrow at the community centre in work clothes.' He smiled at the woman. 'Not that we're both as head-over-

37

heels as we used to be.'

The woman asked if he loved the Starfish Bride and he said of course he did. He also loved peace and quiet. He also loved the woman's name; where was it from?

The woman and the Starfish Groom drank some warm sodas from the mini kitchen, sat on the edge of the white tailor's round which was bare of dresses, talked about their very different childhoods (his rich, hers poor) and he put his hand in her hair.

'Where did all that pain go?' he said. 'Is it here?' He placed his thumb next to her eyes. 'Or here.' He put his thumb in her mouth.

The woman realised she was pregnant with the child of the Starfish Groom a month after they had sex on the tailor's round. Her very regular period was gone. She was feeling bent out of shape, like soft clay that was being pulled piece by piece, like a tangled thatch of wire.

By this time, the Starfish Bride was a forgotten topic of conversation at Celestial Diamond, replaced by the Chinese retailers who were refusing to refund the imports that had shown up water-logged and rusted. The Starfish Bride would be married by the end of spring. The woman quit her job without fanfare, returned to her mother's house and gave birth to Nona.

'At least she has a mother,' her mother had said. 'A child needs a mother more than a father.'

After the birth the woman had been bedridden for three weeks. Catching a delirious fever, seeing visions of herself, imagining thunder. Her dreams conjured her own father, who she was supposed to need less. She cried silently to herself.

She knew where all the pain went: into the things she had made.

Nona was healthy, but quiet, sensitive to hard touches and loud sounds. She wailed for breast milk when she was moved to formula, spitting up with violent, shuddering undulations. Her watery eyes were always accusing the woman of something; sometimes the woman apologised without knowing why.

The woman found a job as a factory runner forty minutes away, lived in a bunk bed with foreigners and wandering souls like herself until she could afford a small Dell laptop. The woman launched her career as a professional liar, told her mother that the best place for her to be was Kuala Lumpur; that's where all the money was and the Wi-Fi in the village was no good.

The woman wants to write reviews of herself to her daughter. Your mother tries to be a good person, she is a hard worker, she is resourceful, she was born under certain unfortunate stars. You should love her! You should not be angry! You should give her a chance! As if any of this would make the years up to Nona, as if Nona won't become a woman who has 'a story to tell' about her mother. As if her reputation can be saved.

The woman scours the website of The Smiling Fish for images of the Starfish Groom, but sees only the Starfish Bride on the About Us page. Divorced, maybe? After only eight years? She wonders what became of the underwater wedding, as it seems the Starfish Bride still has an affinity for the deep.

The woman writes a short email that takes a few hours to construct. She makes a cup of instant coffee as the merbau bounce up and down, a few hanging pots crash into the alley.

She writes to say that she is happy to run a trial period for The Smiling Fish, it depends what they're after, her area of expertise lies in online reputation management, she puts out positive reviews for a certain price. As far as a restaurant goes, Google would surely be the site to concentrate efforts on. The woman attaches a few stats to the email to prove her point.

For the rest of the day, the woman waits for a response. She makes pancakes for dinner and she begins another letter to her mother. In the pile of ripped envelopes, folded notes and old letters, she finds the poem that Nona wrote in English. Her mother had cut it from Nona's schoolbook, including where the teacher had written 'PROMISING!'

> *She lives under the mountain*
> *The mountain is a cloud*
> *The mountain is wet*
> *She falls in the water*
> *She cries under the mountain*

Each word 'mountain' is written in capital letters with a red pen. That had been the 'word of the day'. The woman wonders if it is Nona who is under the mountain.

The Starfish Bride writes back under her maiden name, which the woman now remembers, and asks for an example review that can be posted for free, in good faith, so that she can gauge the woman's talent for English. If the review lands well, she will ask for further reviews and a site optimisation.

The woman, as she does before every review, thinks about who she wants to be. What would 'land' well with the Starfish Bride and any potential reader? Who is she writing for? What would she want to hear?

The woman peels herself off the couch to close the curtains. The rain has stopped, the sky has faded into a quietness that promises a milder morning. The humidity has risen, the threat will soon be green, the birds will return, the merbau will regrow flowers and more flowers.

The woman writes her final review, thinking only of who she wants to be.

> *My family and I really enjoyed our time at The Smiling Fish. Excellent table service and the grilled mackerel was especially good! I recommend getting out of the house now that the storm is fading and the danger is finally over. Eat the grilled mackerel even if you hate fish and you're allergic and will die soon afterwards. Spend your last few moments on Earth doing something that surprises you. Give up your name and you'll regret it. I have a daughter and her name is Nona and she has your husband's eyes and my mother's love of poetry. They have something for everyone at The Smiling Fish. Five fucking stars.*

Sugar

Nayela Wickramasuriya

Colombo is peaceful at this time in the morning. We start school at 7:30 and it takes me half an hour to walk there. The roads are quiet, with only a handful of tuk-tuks and the occasional bus. I pick up a large, orange coconut from the man in the tiny kade on the corner and sip the thambili through a white-and-green-striped straw as I hug the sides of the streets, sticking to the shade. My achchi, my mother's mother, has started complaining, saying I'm growing dark from playing in the sun. Boys date fair girls like Shermalee. Her mother is English, her father from Kandy. People from Kandy are the most beautiful in Sri Lanka, with small noses and light eyes. Shermalee does not have light eyes but she has skin like burnt sugar and hair more brown than black. Achchi used to pinch the bridge of my nose to make it thinner but she gave up on my thirteenth birthday. 'Nothing can be done now, baba. Perhaps you will grow into it.' Two years later she still says this.

As I near the school I can see them waiting under the tree, two thin figures in identical uniforms and hair ribbons. My best friends. My mother jokes that we are the Three Musketeers. Minusha is even darker than I am and, from a distance, looks

43

like Shermalee's shadow, their heads bowed close together. I hear her laugh, like a champagne glass dropped on the floor, and wave. She nudges Shermalee who turns and smiles her wide, generous smile. They step apart, making room for me, linking arms and putting me in the middle.

Our classmates have started chasing boys, pinning up the hems of their skirts to shorten them while they walk to and from school. I look at the other girls and feel sad for them, not having friends like Shermalee and Minusha, having to chase boys. I get nervous when my skirt is higher than my knees.

Our first class is history. We are studying Dutugemunu and Elara with Miss Wanigasooriya. She is young and wears brightly coloured saris with contrasting pottus. Today she is wearing a rich green-and-blue sari with an embroidered gold edge and a zigzag pattern on the fall. Her pottu is orange and she looks like a peacock that has been turned into a woman by magic. Miss Wanigasooriya is one of the best teachers. She is kind and beautiful and you can hear her coming because her bangles tinkle when she walks. We have seen her in Green Cabin before, sitting in a booth alone and reading while eating chocolate cake. She lets us join her and asks us questions about what we want to do in life, tells us that we do not just have to get married. She taught us about why it is important that we changed from being called Ceylon to Sri Lanka last year. The other teachers don't like Miss Wanigasooriya. I heard Mrs Jayasinghe the other day saying that Miss Wanigasooriya is asking for it in her fancy saris and walking about Colombo alone. She said that she doesn't know who Miss Wanigasooriya thinks she is to be doing things like that.

Shermalee says that Miss Wanigasooriya is free. She and

Minusha do not want to get married. Shermalee wants to be a dancer and Minusha wants to be a scientist. I sit quietly when they talk about marriage. It makes my throat tighten up and I feel my face get hot. My mother's sister, Aunty Nilmini, did not get married. She was a nurse and used to work late at the hospital. Now she lives with us. Aunty Nilmini is fat and spends her days sitting on the veranda in the hansi putuwa, wearing big batik dresses that are like tents and chewing betel. When she smiles her mouth looks like it is filled with blood.

At noon we take our lunch boxes and sit in the shade of the banyan tree in the playground. We sit on pieces of newspaper, so the red earth does not colour our uniforms, the sunlight dappled through the leaves. Minusha says the tree must be hundreds of years old. It is wide enough that we cannot wrap our arms around it, even when we only touch fingertips.

'Let's try again!' she shrieks, clapping her hands. Shermalee and I jump to attention, giggling and pretending to be serious. 'Maybe we've grown now.'

We face the tree. I lean in and press myself against its cool weight, the bark rough and uneven on my cheek. I can just feel Minusha's fingertips with my left hand, but the distance is still too far and I cannot touch Shermalee. We stretch and strain, laughing and sweating with the effort. Shermalee laughs so hard she spits on the tree and we fall away, holding our sides. I straighten up and Shermalee draws Minusha round her side of the tree by the hand, tears rolling down their faces.

'I guess we're still not big enough. Now give me some of your kalu dodol!'

45

Shermalee hands both me and Minusha a slice. I hold it in my palm where it jiggles gently, black peppered with white cashew nuts. It melts like ice on my tongue, the silky sweetness blooming in my mouth. Clouds twist and unfurl against a vivid-blue sky.

It is a Monday, so after school we have elocution class. The mid-afternoon sun beats down on us and we hide under our brown-paper-wrapped exercise books held over our heads. We pass Perera & Sons and go in to get kimbula banis. The bread is fresh from the oven, chewy and thick, and the large sugar granules on top dissolve in the heat.

Aunty Christine is our elocution teacher and she is old. Her eyes are dark brown with misty grey rings around the irises and her skin crinkles like tissue paper when she smiles at us. She allows us to sit in the garden, eating our kimbula banis before class.

Uncle Alfred is there and is choosing his crabs today. He tells the crab boy to empty his burlap sack at the end of the garden. The crabs tumble out one after the other, making gentle thudding noises as they hit the grass. Their dark blue-green colour stands out against the blazing, fat-bladed lawn. At first, they are confused. I think if they had eyelids, they would blink.

'Come, girls, you can help me.'

We rise, brushing sugar from our skirts, and take our places on either side of the crabs, forming a path. The crab boy pokes at them with a flimsy stick. They start to run. Uncle moves around us, pointing at the crabs that are the most alive, running the fastest. He chooses eight and the crab boy plucks them off the grass, dropping them into a large, pale-pink bucket. His skin is almost black under the holes in his grey-white T-shirt; it reminds me of a Dalmatian dog that I saw in a book once.

As he passes, Shermalee asks him if he wants a piece of her kimbula banis. The whites of his eyes are bright hoops, his mouth a straight line as he looks at her, then Minusha, then me. Shermalee breaks off a piece and holds it out to him. He takes a step closer and extends his hand, palm flat so she doesn't have to touch him when she gives it to him. He smells like the sea.

The next day, I drop my inkwell at the end of the period just before lunch and stay back to clean up as Mrs Jayasinghe watches.

'Hurry up, child! Delaying mealtimes is very bad for the digestion!'

I put the tissues in the bin and watch Mrs Jayasinghe hurrying down the hall, the fat of her back spilling out around the edges of her too-tight blouse.

Shermalee and Minusha are sitting under the tree when I arrive. Shermalee has puhul dosi today. The pale-cream chunks are the same colour as the sugar and egg whites our maid Kanthi beats together when she makes meringue. They feel like treasures, heavy and cool in our hands and teeth as we bite into the gelatinous sweetness. This is the only time I like pumpkin.

Minusha is looking at Shermalee, her mouth twisted sideways into a mischievous smile. She sees me looking.

'Shermalee had her first kiss the other day.' The words burst from her like pulp from a mango squeezed too hard.

'Aiyo, it's not just me! You had your first kiss the other day too!'

47

They are both looking at me and I have an emptiness in my belly rising to my mouth. I try to breathe in and find that the air around me has solidified. A kiss. Two kisses. One for each of them and I did not know.

'I thought you said we didn't need boys!' Minusha edges backwards and I know that my voice was too loud. 'When? Why didn't you tell me?'

Shermalee reaches out and puts her hand on my arm, her tea-with-milk skin cool against mine. 'It was only at the weekend. For both of us. We just wanted to try and see. But we will always be your friends. We didn't say because we weren't sure if you would tell Headmistress Gunadasa.'

Tears prick my eyes, blurring my vision. 'I would never tell.'

Shermalee smiles at me, her face soft and open. 'I know.'

'Are you going to do it again? Which boys?'

They grin at each other and Minusha shrugs. 'Oh, just some fellows we know through Shermy's cousin. Why not? It was fun. Let's see.' She nibbles at her puhul dosi and Shermalee draws shapes in the dust with her heel.

That afternoon I cannot concentrate on my reading or my drawing.

On Sunday night I am jolted awake just before midnight, though I do not know by what. The air is thick and syrupy after the heavy rains and my fan moves overhead as if through treacle. I fumble in the dark and open the door to the bathroom, sitting down on the commode and willing myself to urinate. My parents are downstairs and their voices carry in the quiet.

'What a thing, so shocking.' My mother. It sounds like

Colombo gossip so I strain to catch what they are saying.

'What are they saying happened?'

'She was out walking, not even so late, you know. Must have been seven or so. She was walking near Independence Square. Three men in a tuk-tuk grabbed her and dragged her in, took her down Torrington Avenue.'

'No one heard? She didn't scream?'

'Must have covered her mouth. Luckily, after they finished, they left her on Keppetipola Mawatha. Some people found her and took her straight to Joseph Fraser.'

'What a sin. This is that young one, no?'

'Yes, very attractive also. This is what happens if girls walk alone at night.'

'Mmm, must be careful these days.' The ice cubes in my father's whisky clink gently against the glass.

'So what about this wedding next weekend?'

'What to do so, can't not go.'

I lie in bed, wondering what happened and to whom until sleep presses down on me once more.

The next day the school is buzzing like a hive. Girls are clustered in hallways, standing in groups and talking in lowered voices. I look for Minusha and Shermalee and cannot find them, so move through the crowds scanning them for Shermalee. I see her at the end of a long corridor, standing out like a pearl in the sea of dark faces. Minusha is by her side, holding her hand, and they are speaking with our classmates in hushed tones.

Minusha grasps my elbow and I can feel her nails digging into the soft skin in the crease of my arm. 'Have you heard?'

'Have I heard what?'

'Your parents didn't tell you?'

'No. What is happening?'

Shermalee opens her mouth to speak when Headmistress Gunadasa appears at the top of the stairs. 'Everybody to the chapel. Now!'

Tears spill down Shermalee's face, leaving silvery trails on her cheeks.

We crowd into the chapel, a kind of order taking shape amongst the chaos. Girls pile onto the pews in a mix of forms, older girls muddled with younger ones and prefects herding people into the nearest seat. Minusha, Shermalee and I hold on to each other's uniforms in the throng and manage to sit together. Shermalee is in the middle and takes my and Minusha's hands. The teachers flank us along the sides of the chapel, lining the walls.

'Girls, silence!' Headmistress Gunadasa's voice rings across us like a bell and the silence is immediate.

'I have some very bad news. I can see that some of you have already heard. But for those who have not, I am very sad to say that Miss Wanigasooriya will not be returning to teach here.' Headmistress Gunadasa waits for the gasps to subside before continuing. 'There was a very unfortunate incident on Saturday night and Miss Wanigasooriya is in hospital. She will be there for some time and we expect her recovery will take many months. In the meantime, this is a good opportunity for me to remind you not to walk around alone. You must always be in groups. Do not wear lots of make-up or jewellery. Do not wear fancy clothes. If you behave modestly and keep your heads down then nothing bad will happen to you.'

Mrs Jayasinghe is leaning against the end of the pew and I hear her mutter: 'Terrible, but I must say I'm not surprised.'

Minusha swivels in her seat and glares at her, and Mrs Jayasinghe shrinks and looks away.

We do not study for the rest of the day. For some lessons, the teachers do not even come to the classrooms, leaving us to push desks together and discuss what had happened.

'Miss was my favourite teacher,' says Anarkali, chewing on the end of her single, dark braid.

'You don't have to talk about her in the past tense, Anarkali,' snaps Minusha. 'Miss hasn't died, she's just in hospital.'

'I'd want to die if someone did that to me.'

'But why? It wouldn't be your fault! She was just going for an evening walk. It's not a crime.' Minusha's face is ablaze. I see Shermalee put her hand gently on her leg under the desk, but Minusha ignores it.

'Who will marry her now?' Anarkali's braid hangs moist over her left shoulder.

'Miss didn't want to get married!' Minusha's hands are shaking on the desk. 'She wanted to teach and go abroad and do things!'

'She can still do those things, Minu.'

Minusha turns to Shermalee and her face softens. 'I know.'

I can feel the heat rising up my neck as I ready myself to ask: 'What happened to her?' I can feel a dozen pairs of eyes on me, whites showing, silence filling the gaps between us like oil.

Minusha leans forward on her elbows so she can look past Shermalee, at me.

'She was raped.'

*

After school that day, Shermalee's father meets us at the gate and we walk together to her house. Uncle has never picked us up before and Shermalee holds his hand. Minusha and I are walking behind them and her hands are hanging by her sides. I watch her left hand, wondering whether I should take it. She sees me looking and pulls her satchel off her shoulder, holding it in the space between us. My palms prickle and we walk in silence.

Shermalee's mother, Aunty Shirley, who insists that we call her just Shirley, is from England. She is the tallest of all the mothers at school. She has pale-blue eyes and fine, straw-coloured hair that falls around her shoulders. I once found a strand of it caught on my satchel buckle. It felt thin between my fingers, a silken thread that would break under the slightest force. I burned it with the candle in my bedroom. It shrivelled against the heat of the flame, filling the air with a strange, sour smell.

We sit in Shermalee's room and Aunty Shirley brings us fresh passion-fruit juice in tall glasses. Minusha has barely said a word since lunch and I am beginning to sweat under my arms. Shermalee pulls out her box of marbles. She has the biggest collection I have ever seen. The marbles they have in the UK are much better than the ones we have here. My favourite one is the size of an eyeball. I saw an eyeball once, in a rotten dead dog by the side of the road. It had been hit by a car and its jaw was broken sideways. We had stopped for a thambili on a long drive back from Galle and I saw its smashed face in the ditch, its eyeball hanging out of the socket. This marble is the same size. It is clear with a bright-yellow twist inside. When I spin the marble on the floor the twist dances and blurs into a single shape, making the whole marble look yellow. When it is still, it looks like a fish.

Shermalee and Minusha are talking in hushed voices.

'Don't you have any opinions?'

I look up to see that Minusha is watching me and I start sweating again.

'I don't know. What happened was bad.'

'What happened was bad? That's it? It was bad?'

I can tell from the look on Shermalee's face that I have said the wrong thing. A bead of liquid runs down my spine and I think of what Headmistress Gunadasa said.

'But this is why they tell us to wear skirts to our knees and not to wear lots of make-up and jewellery. If we do, we are drawing attention to ourselves and obviously bad things happen!'

'We should not be teaching girls what to wear. We should be teaching boys not to rape.' Minusha's stare cracks like a whip. I look at Shermalee for support, but she has turned away from me and is sorting the marbles by colour.

Minusha stands and walks to Shermalee's bedroom door.

'If you ask Shirley she will drop you home.'

As I stand on the outside of the closed door I can hear their voices pitching up and down but I cannot make out what they are saying.

The next day in maths class Minusha and Shermalee sit in different seats at the front. Anarkali sits next to them so I sit at the back in my usual seat. I find it difficult to think.

At lunch I go out to the tree but they are not there. The spaces where we usually sit between the roots are empty. My throat feels tight. I try to swallow my food, drinking warm water from my metal canteen, but the lump at the base of my neck does not move. There are girls around me sitting in groups but no one asks me to join them. Oil from my lunch mottles my palms, filling the whorls on my fingertips with an orange tinge.

I cannot eat and wrap up the patties in the napkin Kanthi gave me. On the walk home I feed them to the three-legged dog by the kade. He looks at me with gratitude, his bedraggled tail sweeping a half-moon in the dust.

The following day Minusha and Shermalee are sitting at the back but Minusha has put her bag on my seat. She glares at me when I start walking to join them, so I sit at the front next to Anarkali.

On the way out, Shermalee drops a note on my desk as I stand.

Come to my house after dinner.

I eat lunch in Miss Wanigasooriya's empty classroom. Mrs Jayasinghe peers through the little glass window in the door, her bulbous eyes poking over the bottom of the pane. I watch her looking at me and she hesitates for a moment before walking down the corridor, the folds of her sari hissing.

When I get to Shermalee's house later there is a power cut. I clutch my satchel as I inch up the wooden slatted stairs. My toes ache from gripping the stalk of my Bata slippers. I reach the landing and I can hear Shermalee's and Minusha's voices, low in the night. As I near the door I can see them sitting on the bed, hazy through the mint-green mesh of Shermalee's mosquito net. Shermalee is cross-legged in the middle of the bed and Minusha has the leg nearer Shermalee tucked under her, leaving the other trailing on the floor.

'Aiyo, Shermy, I don't know why you've insisted on this.

What are we bothering with her for? She has no opinions! She repeats what she's told, like that mynah at the kade.'

My legs feel like they are held up by strings.

'Minu, don't be cruel. She doesn't have any other friends.'

'But she is so weird!'

'Minu.' Shermalee reaches out and tucks Minusha's jet-black hair behind her ear. 'She is good for us. We need her.'

My heart swells. Shermalee has always been kind to me. She has always been my friend, ever since we were little.

Shermalee's hand is on the nape of Minusha's neck. 'If we have her around, we can spend more time together, without anyone thinking anything. She will never suspect.'

Minusha lifts her face to smile at Shermalee. She reaches out, crooks her index finger and uses it to tip Shermalee's chin towards her. They move their faces closer together and –

I dart away from the door with such force that I knock into the table behind me, sending a brass bowl flying. The clang reverberates, circling the landing over and over as I fumble about in the dark. The bed creaks and Shermalee and Minusha appear in the doorway.

'What are you doing?'

'I'm sorry, I couldn't see, I knocked the bowl.' I feel sick and keep swallowing as I crawl on the floor.

Shermalee runs around the table holding a candle. She crouches and puts her cool hand on my arm, her eyes twinkling as she smiles at me. 'Don't worry. I will find it in the morning.'

Minusha is still standing in the doorway, arms folded over her chest. Her cheekbones cut into the darkness and I cannot see her eyes.

We sit on the bed afterwards and Shermalee and Minusha

are laughing, but I do not notice what they say. They touch each other again and again and my skin burns as I watch them. Shermalee has jalebis as a special treat. I hold the cluster of golden rings in my hand and when I bite into it the syrup spills into my mouth. It is too sweet. Heat builds in my stomach and between my legs and I feel hot, choked in the night, as if I have spent too long in the sun.

After some time, I do not know how long, I ask Uncle to drop me home. Shirley comes for the drive, holding her fair arm out of the window while she talks about how she prefers Colombo at night. She says the darkness holds secrets and she and Uncle exchange a look before laughing.

When I reach home I lie on my bed and try to squeeze tears from my eyes, but no matter how hard I try they will not come.

I wake the next morning bathed in sweat. My sheets are damp and my nightdress clings to my body. My mother comes in to see why I have not gone downstairs for breakfast and immediately decides that I should not go to school. She brings a wet towel to lay on my forehead and I shiver under the fan cranking above me. When I sleep, I dream of Minusha's finger under Shermalee's chin.

The day after that I am still sick. I have not eaten and barely kept down the thambili Kanthi brought to my bedside. Sometime in the afternoon, my mother knocks on my door. Minusha and Shermalee have come to see me. I tell my mother I am too sick to see them. I hear their voices faintly through the door and my mother brings me a small plate. On it are two slices of love cake Shermalee has brought. The sickly almond smell creeps into my nostrils and I ask Kanthi to take it away.

On the third day, I feel a bit better, but my mother insists that I stay home. I do not want to go outside. When I think of Minusha's crooked finger my skin prickles, invisible fingernails scraping up my neck, the hairs on my arms standing up like soldiers.

'Amma!'

My mother walks in, holding a book.

'Amma, I have something I need to tell you. It's about Minusha and Shermalee.'

'What happened?'

'I saw them –' My voice snags on the back of my throat, like a fish on a hook.

'You saw them what?'

My mouth is dry, my lips cracked. I try to find the words.

'Kissing,' I stutter.

'You saw them kissing who?'

My eyes are streaming, but I am not crying.

My mother repeats her question. 'Which boys was it? Who did you see them kissing?' I can see heat spreading up my mother's neck. Her skin reddens when she is angry.

'Each other. I saw them kissing each other. They do things together. They touch each other and put their hands in their clothes and they pretend they are friends but they are not.' I feel like I am vomiting. 'They kiss in private, that is why they are always at each other's houses. They are not interested in boys.'

My mother's face is ashen. 'You stay here.'

I lie on my back and listen to the sound of the telephone dial going round.

By the time I return, I have missed two weekends and seven

whole days of school, the longest I have ever been absent. I feel excited, as if it is the start of a new school year.

Minusha and Shermalee are missing from maths, history and English. I eat alone under the banyan tree.

Four weeks later, Minusha returns to school. She sits at the front of maths class, Shermalee's desk empty beside her. People whisper when she walks in but no one talks to her. At lunch, I find her sitting in the dirt beneath the tree, red soil on her white uniform. As I approach she looks up and I can see she is crying.

'How could they send her away like that?'

I pretend to be confused.

'What do you mean?'

'Shermalee! Her parents sent her to some school in England. She has gone there with her mother. I have been writing to her but she hasn't replied. She hasn't written to me once.'

We sit in silence, the sunlight spiking through the leaves.

'Do you want me to come to your house after school, Minusha?'

She nods slowly, her hair falling over her face.

Before going to Minusha's that afternoon, I go home to get the pack of letters that Shermalee has sent to me. Among the many pages, only one was for me, telling me to give the rest to Minusha. Shermalee said she could not send them to Minusha herself because of a 'misunderstanding'.

When I reach her house, Minusha is sitting on her bed, weeping silently into a snotty, damp handkerchief. Her hair is tangled and the flesh around her eyes is red and swollen, blending into her cheeks. I feel sorry for her. She is disgusting now, like food that has rotted.

The tinkle of the bombai muttai man's bell filters through the window from the street. 'Come, Minu, let's eat some bombai muttai.' She shakes her head. I run down the stairs and into the street, waving the man down. He is old and barely taller than me, a white sarong with horizontal coloured stripes wrapped around his stick-thin legs. I drop the coins into his palm and he hands me a portion of delicate pink floss. It feels like a fistful of hair in the thin plastic bag.

Upstairs I break off a piece and hand it to Minusha. She holds it in her hands, head bowed. Tears melt the sugar where they fall. I pull off a long chunk and fold it onto itself, then stuff it into my mouth. The strands blur, flowing over my tongue, down my throat, across my skin. Thick white clouds churn across a sky that is beginning to turn the same peachy pink colour as the bombai muttai in our hands.

The crickets are beginning to sing outside. She says nothing, does not eat her bombai muttai, even though I went down and bought it for her with my own money.

'Minusha? It will be OK.'

She looks at me.

'You don't understand. We loved each other more than anyone else.'

I can hear my heart beating.

I finish my half of the bombai muttai and stand, picking strands of it off my skirt. I drop them out of the window, so the ants don't come in. Minusha's face is tilted downwards again, the bombai muttai a clumped mess in her lap. I tell her that if I get any post from Shermalee I will bring it straight to her.

Outside, I drop the letters in her neighbour's garbage.

The afternoon heat is lifting as the evening comes in. I pin up the hem of my skirt and walk home, feeling the breeze on my knees.

Donal

JP Pangilinan-O'Brien

Fucks sake, man. Three times. It's easy. Like this.

Donal drops the ball onto his foot and it springs back to the creases in his hips and down again.

You're not giving me the right kinda ball, I say.

He throws his hands up in protest. Get ta fuck, he says. What kind of other ball could I give you?

We're on Donal's estate. My aunt lives here too, but we're on Donal's part of it. He lives here with his dad, from Dublin, and his ma, from Poland. They don't get along, but me and Donal don't talk much about that.

Send it up, I say. It lands on my foot before careening off to the side.

You're shite, Donal says, laughing.

Donal's house is one from the end, starting from the left, on the top half of the estate. It is high up, circled by mountains, and the weather is either terrible or glorious, nothing in between. He lives next to the Mulahey kids, but we don't play with them. We caught the younger one, the boy with thick glasses, taking his hand on and off the electric fence for the cattle last summer. When we asked him what the fuck he was at, he said he was only playing.

Donal's house is small. They keep the curtains closed, and were it not for the smoke rising out of the chimney, you might think it was empty. The inside of the house is tidy and organised. Both of Donal's parents smoke, but they make a big deal of emptying the ashtray after every cigarette.

How come you don't draw the curtains? I say.

My dad says those Mulahey kids are always looking in at him.

I feign outrage. Disgrace, I say.

Sometimes, if we're lucky, my aunt will leave cans of Bulmers in the fridge. I put them in my bag and take the back door out to the garden, up over the wall, where Donal is waiting. We cross the road leading out of the estate and walk through the long grass to the pitch.

Where's your da anyway? he asks.

In the Philippines, I say.

Is that next to China?

I don't think so.

Don't you talk to him?

Not really, I say.

Good man yourself, he says. I wouldn't talk to my da either if I had the chance.

My aunt knows Donal's dad. She lifts her hand off the wheel to salute him when they drive past each other, and sometimes they'll even stop side by side and roll down the windows. How are ya, Declan? she'll say. Then, when he drives away, she'll shake her head. Terrible drinker that man. I don't reply, but I know she's right. There have been times when me and Donal have found him in the pitch black, tracing invisible walls on the path up from the village. One time we followed him and whispered his name, hiding behind cars. Just before the turn-off for our road, he spun around and shouted Cunt! into the darkness before falling into a ditch.

Donal is from Dublin, but he came to Kerry as a kid. Even though he's spent all this time here, he considers Kerry folk uncouth. The only time I've seen him and his dad get along is when they tell jokes about Kerry men. They like to sit on their wall overlooking the road and stare down at the uncivilised masses. One time the father of the Mulahey kids overheard them, and Donal's dad had to speak to him outside his gate while me and Donal snatched glances from behind the curtain.

We're three weeks into summer when I turn thirteen. Donal tells me his dad has tickets for the quarter-finals in Tralee, and asks if I want to go as a present. We're going to blow them out of it, he says. Kerry, that is. When the Mulahey kid's ball rolls down to us, he kicks it into the field below instead of sending it up to him. Get ta fuck, he says, punching the air. We watch the kid run past us, and Donal nods as though it is a good omen. I go home that evening and tell my aunt that we have tickets for the quarter-finals. She says she'll let me go so long as there's no drinking. I promise there won't be.

We leave in the morning in his dad's van. I sit on the left of Donal. He crushes me against the window when his dad speeds up on the bends.

Do you smoke, Jesse? Donal's dad says.

I tell him I don't.

Fair fucks, he says, lighting up a cigarette.

We stop halfway to Tralee for petrol. Donal's dad asks if we'd like a packet of Taytos. I don't want to be rude, so I wait until Donal says yes before adding my approval. When his dad gets back, he has a bag full of cans. For the game, he says, winking. We speed the rest of the way to Tralee, and I can hear the soft dent of aluminium when the cans collide on the way there.

We don't make it for the first half. Donal's dad meets someone he used to work with in the pub across from the ground, and the two of them stand at the bar until the game starts. Me and Donal stand outside, drinking 7UP, until he starts murmuring under his breath and grows pink in the face. I watch him barge through the crowd of adults until he gets to his father. I can't hear what they say to each other, but it's only Donal's dad and his friend who are laughing when the conversation stops. Come on, Donal says when he comes out. We go in for the second half. As soon as we pass the turnstiles, the crowd is so loud that it becomes a current that pulsates through the walls and into the floor beneath us. Kerry are good. They send the ball back and forth to each other in perfectly shaped arcs. Dublin trail the whole game. When we get out, we have to call Donal's mum to pick us up because his dad is too pissed to drive.

The next day Donal asks to see a picture of my father. I tell him I don't have one, but then he says we should search for him on Facebook. When we find his profile, Donal spends five minutes asking me who all the other people in the photos with him are, and he isn't pleased when I tell him that I don't know.

C'mere, he says. Another thing. I think you were wrong about it not being close to China.

There is not much to do in the country. Sometimes Malley, a kid who lives on the top of the hill, comes down to visit us.

He is skinny like me, but he has strong calves from running cross-country. We walk. When we get to the farmer's field, Malley calls me a pussy. You wouldn't run across that field, he says. The bull will catch you. I tell him he doesn't know what he's talking about, but I jump straight off the fence when the bull raises his head and starts walking towards us.

There is a sea after the hill. We don't choose the easy way there, the road replaced by upward fields and the lanes that zigzag through them. We make our way to the top, and three-quarters of the way there the wind is so loud we stop talking. I can hear my heart beating through my ears. It is a clear day, the sky a singular sheet of blue, and we can make out the small details of houses in nearby parishes. The sun pushes down on our shoulders. We should go swimming, Donal shouts.

The path down is long. It twists between red and purple bushes, and we take a moment to sit in the shade of overhanging branches. When we get to the beach, we are panting like dogs. Malley's cousin owns the store next to the car park, so he gets us a drink and we sit on the benches outside the café watching the crowds.

Last summer, Malley says, my cousin rode some girl from Kilkenny.

He did not, says Donal.

He did. Took her out past those dunes, he says, and rode her.

Donal looks at me, but I stare out towards the sea. I don't know anything about girls, not enough to pretend, anyway.

Hope he didn't get her pregnant, Donal says.

Malley laughs. Get ta fuck, he says. She was the one who had the condom, like.

We sit there for a bit, listening to the ocean. Then Malley gets up and says the last person into the sea has to suck their dad's dick, so we all sprint head first towards the shore, leaving an unbroken line of clothes behind us. We only slow down when we reach the jagged edge of broken pebbles, and, even then, we pigeon-foot our way forward, wincing through the pain. The water is cold. I throw myself under and kick. When I come up again, the sun has left parcels of light on the waves. Every so often, I have to duck under the surf and underneath it tastes of salt and the dark. After one wave, I see Malley bobbing up and down and pointing out towards the horizon. I follow him, and we swim beside one another. Every time I turn to my left and see him there, I feel as though I am putting coins into a jar that I will one day use. Two minutes and we are out further than anyone on the beach. The waves are no longer obtrusive but squeeze past us, rippling around our legs. Race you back, Malley says, and he doesn't give me a chance to start alongside him because he is gone the moment he says it.

I follow him in and, halfway to the shore, see Donal. I realise he has not come with us to the sea's limits. I swim over and when I am close, I see that he is shaking.

Donal, I say. Are you all right?

I move closer still and realise that he is standing, that we are far enough in now to put our feet on the silk of the sand underneath. I am about to tell him he should go in if he's cold, but then I realise that he is crying. Sobbing, really. I put a hand on his shoulder but he pulls away from me and tells me to fuck off. Let's go in, I say, but he shakes his head and I don't know what to do so I continue swimming back. He stays there for what feels like twenty minutes, the waves

66

crashing over him. He does not walk straight over to us when he comes out of the water, and I watch him move through the crowds of people like a stray dog. His eyes are red when he comes back, but Malley pretends not to notice so I do the same.

Donal's father buys a computer and installs it in their front room. He has become obsessed with eBay, particularly the buying and selling of miniature cars. For this, he must use Donal as a go-between, since he is the only one who understands the demands of an internet browser. This is a blessing and a curse. Donal helps him, but he learns more than his father would like. He knows all the passwords, and soon we start siphoning small amounts of money to Donal's credit union account. We plan to buy Liverpool shirts. On the days when we get tired of my feet and their clumsiness with the ball, we go into Donal's room and stare at his deposit book.

One evening we go down to the village to watch United play. There are older boys in the pub, and Donal asks one of them to buy us a pint. It works and the two of us sit in the corner of a booth, craning our necks to get an angle where we can see the game and not be caught by the barman. Donal speaks to the other kids about transfers and competitions across continents, none of which I can match. Other than this, it is a quiet affair. But five minutes into the second half, Donal's father emerges through the doors. He is swaying, throwing his hand out to steady himself against the bar when he orders.

United are losing. Donal and his father are Liverpool supporters, of course, and so this doesn't bother them much.

His father is particularly animated at the team's misfortunes. He speaks to the barman about his friends in Dublin who were United fans and their stinginess. They'd make you buy a pint at your own father's funeral, he says. He is getting louder and louder, but people do not stare. Whether this is because they are used to Donal's father or because Donal himself is here, I do not know. With ten minutes to go, United bring on Park Ji-sung and Donal's father announces that they are subbing the chink on. I look around, but no one seems to be bothered.

Did you hear what your dad said? I ask Donal on the walk home.

I did, yeah. He was acting the bollix.

I feel heartened by this, and I turn with a smile.

Not that he's wrong, he says.

What?

United fans, he says. They're the worst. I just wish he wasn't so fucking loud all the time.

I say nothing.

When we get back home, I turn on my aunt's laptop and search for my father. I read the Wikipedia page on the Philippines, and press the speaker button underneath the words on the entry on Tagalog. The voice is robotic. I press it so many times that my aunt bangs on the wall and tells me to go easy. I think about how I cannot remember what my father sounds like, or how he smells. It is late, past midnight, when I cry.

We don't ever get to buy the shirts because Donal's father finds out he has been stealing from him. I don't see Donal for three days. When he finally does come out, he has purple and yellow bruises on his arms which he covers with a jumper the day after I ask him about them. Malley's grandmother lives on the estate, so we hang out when he comes down. It rains heavy that week, huge drops of rain that leave streaks of grey on our faces from where the gel has dissolved. We take cover in the doorways of neighbours who we have never spoken to before.

One day, on a walk to the lake, we come across a farmer's field with sheep. Malley dares Donal to throw a rock. When Donal starts he does not stop. The rocks land with a thud, and we both tell him to stop when we realise the sheep is caught against the fence and cannot move. It is wailing, making that sound that animals do when they lose a child. Malley pulls Donal's hand when he cocks it back, and when the rock lands on the ground, Donal turns around and lets him have it. There is a crack. Malley cradles his nose in his hands. I watch the blood run through the space between his fingers. When we look up, Donal is running away and my dreams later that night are filled with the coarse sound of gravel underfoot.

I walk up to the field the next morning and the sheep is dead. Its head is caved in from the rock, and it feels strange to watch the flies gather at the cavity whilst the birds sing overhead. I stand up on the fence to get a closer look, but then I hear what I think is the sound of a gate opening in a distant field and I run, thinking it's the farmer. When I get back, my aunt is awake and she tells me my flight home is in a week. I go up to Donal's house to tell him. He is playing games in his room. He takes the ball from kick-off and runs it back to his own half to score an own goal, but I don't ask him why he is doing it. Of all the stupid questions to ask, this seems the worst. Donal has the lights off and the green of the digital pitch shines neon on our faces.

I'm going next week, I say.

Donal pauses the game. It's been a month already?

That's what my aunt says.

There's going to be nothing to do when you're gone, he says.

Maybe you can come visit me in London.

Yeah, he says, unpausing the game. Maybe.

On my way out, I stop by the living-room door. Donal's dad has left the door ajar. When I look through the gap, I see that he is looking at porn. He has his back to me, but I can see the faces of Asian women in the space between his shoulders and the screen. They are soundless, their heads moving like buoys on open water. I stay still for a second, but then shout goodbye, as if I am walking past, and watch him fumble for the mouse. The keyboard falls and he presses all of the keys, but he has no success in turning the screen off. In fact he has opened a new video, and the audio is on now, getting louder and louder. Donal's mum appears in the corridor.

Everything all right, Jesse? she says.

Yeah, I say, putting on my shoes. I was just saying goodbye.

Details

Leeor Ohayon

I was about a minute away from deleting the app, but then you sent me that message. I'd whittled away the best part of the morning, scrolling through a blur of torsos and silhouettes. We had a good back-and-forth, traded pictures and words in a way that didn't sound like we were haggling over goods at the market.

You said, Can I see more pics?

And I think neither of us was initially convinced. The first pic you sent wasn't bad, the second was hot, but the third and fourth did you no favours.

Instead, it was your human approach which caught my attention, the way you'd waited until the end of our chat to ask what for others are opening questions: What're you looking for? you asked. What're you into?

That day we got talking, I even made an exception and sent you some nudes, which I don't usually do. But I was frustrated enough and determined to get *it*.

You said you could host, that you could do right now, how does in one hour sound?

And I jumped in the shower, got myself ready and fresh, made my way to your altbau, on the Maybachufer, overlooking the canal.

You said, Press Khoury on the doorbell when you get here.

I stood by the front of your block, chewing up my nails, waiting for you to buzz me in.

Told myself, I should have asked for you to walk with me before coming to yours. What if you looked nothing like the pics? What if this is where I met my end?

But then you buzzed me in and I walked through to a corridor, spotless and tidy, not a pizza leaflet in sight. Even the bikes in the courtyard were parked nice and neat. A far cry from the stench and noise that lined – still line – the way to my flat (the one you never got to see).

Told myself that if this was it, at least they'd trace my body back to a respectable place.

I climbed up five flights of stairs, the blood beating in my ears and the thud of my shoes on the stairs making a soundtrack of jitters all the way to your floor. You had left the door ajar for me, and I rested beside it, regaining my composure before I knocked. I fixed a hand through my hair, checked my breath and my pits, waited for my panting to slow, and then you popped your head through the gap. I felt my cheeks burn up as you said to me: Five flights are very exhausting.

As you swung open the door to reveal yourself, I made a joke about it being like an episode of *Stars in their Eyes*, which you didn't understand, told you, Forget it – it's a bad British cultural reference.

So that's where you're from, couldn't remember if it was UK or US, you said in that hard-to-place accent.

And you're from Beirut? I asked and you nodded, urged

me – Shoes off please, come inside.

You wore a tight black T-shirt, the hair on your chest spilling out from the top, and a pair of sport shorts that emphasised the curve of your bum; no doubt you wore them on purpose. You looked better in the flesh than in your pics (usually it's the other way round). And the eye contact you gave, told me you equally liked what you saw.

Something to drink?

I said water would be grand.

You smiled, a comma-like dimple attached at the end.

Just water? you said. I've got juice, I've got beer . . . I've got something stronger?

I'll have whatever you're having?

You said, Two Augustiners coming right up. Living room is on the right.

While you busied yourself with bottle caps, I ran fingers across all that minimalist, clean, Danish teak furniture, stopped by the bookcase in the corner, glanced at the titles in Arabic and French, English and German. Fanon and Said on one shelf, Baldwin and Morrison and Angelou on another, but it was your copy of Kahanoff that caught my eye.

I'm surprised you have this, I said, as soon as you returned. You handed me a beer, and we clinked bottles in silence, locked eyes in customary German. You stood beside me, elbows touching, as we surveyed the contents of your shelves, close enough that I could smell your lemon-mint shower gel.

You proceeded to tease me, asked me with a disarming smile, What's so surprising? That a Lebanese Arab's taken an interest in a Jewish writer?

I stumbled for words, tried to tell you I didn't mean it like

73

that, said, I mentioned before that I'm technically an Arab, my family are Arab-Jews.

And then you laughed, sat yourself down on the sofa, asked me, Are people still using *that*? Kahanoff called herself a Levantine.

I said I knew that.

You said that you liked the term, it allowed for more grey.

What do you mean?

That we're all technically Levantines. Neither here nor there. Neither fully West nor East. I grew up on as much Tupac and Biggie as Fayrouz.

I said to you that I didn't agree, the marketisation of gangsta rap in the nineties isn't exactly an example of cultural symbiosis.

And then you said to me, Oof, those are such big words, and here I was thinking you'd come over just to fuck.

I scratched at my eye as if I had a nervous twitch, unsure how to respond. You beckoned me over to the sofa, and I sat down beside you, knees knocking together.

I'll roll us a joint, you said. Pass me the wooden box under the table.

And you tasked me with making the roach, while you fiddled about with a grinder and skins. You asked me what brought me to Berlin and I told you I was writing my thesis at the Freie.

Shatir, you called me.

Isn't that what you say to kids?

And you laughed, asked me, Bteḥke a'rabe?

I said I knew mostly the swear words, but I could also count to a hundred.

What do you do? I asked.

Software engineer, you said.

And when I tried to prod, find out what that entailed, you told me, Maintaining, managing medical apps.

I handed you the roach, searched your face for cues, like reading words in a language I couldn't speak.

When I asked, When did you move here? you told me you'd been here since you were ten. First Bielefeld, then Berlin, and then fell silent again.

I tapped on my knees, unsure what to do, found your lack of small talk so difficult.

Then you flashed me a smile, asked me, Have you a lighter by the hand?

And I laughed in your face, told you the wording was off. Saw you blush for the first and last time.

The orange embers of the joint flickered as you got it started, and you blew smoke rings to the ceiling as we sank back into the sofa.

Know this? you asked, cranking up the volume on your portable speaker. Not really a question, more of an attempt to impress me.

Mashrou' Leila, I said, and ruined your fun. Told you, I had this album playing on loop, and imparted my knowledge of Lebanese indie and Arabic pop and golden age classics.

You said you were surprised. I said, What's so surprising? That a Jew's taken an interest in Arabic music?

And you laughed, said, Very good.

I said, Besides, it's my culture as well.

You raised your eyebrows.

And I said, My grandparents are from Iraq and Djerba. Where do you think that is, the moon?

But you just smiled, sat there, silent and high. You brushed

75

your pinkie against mine, ever so lightly, almost imperceptible. I waited a full second or two, before I replicated the move, clumsily brushing, something more akin to a twitch. But you understood the message, the green light given. And then all at once, you placed your thick fingers over mine, pressed your lips to my neck and I stiffly surrendered, with the ends of the joint still poised in my other hand.

Images of you stalked me all evening as I waited on tables. I recited to customers the bottles of red that we kept, the specials of the day, as I tried my best to conceal the semi behind my apron. The same scene spun around in my head: us lying there, not really touching, your feet resting on mine, and the smell of lube and sweat and condoms still lingering in the room, as we flowed in and out of conversation on nothing particularly memorable, lounging in those brief few moments before we put on some clothes.

And then you got up, went into your cupboard, threw me a towel in jest, said, Clean yourself up, giggled, and returned to the bed. You watched from your side, head propped in your hands, as I stumbled into my underwear, searching for my T-shirt which had ended up behind the headboard. I flashed you a smile, but you had just turned away, and I told myself it was time to get out.

You asked me my plans for the day.

Told you I'd been hankering after a gemüse kebab, but I might go with a falafel mit erdnuss sauce. And then I added that I'd need a nap before work, as I'm in charge of closing. I told you it had been fun, that the weed was great, steering the conversation towards goodbye. I edged towards the door, struck by the fact that I hadn't felt any post-orgasm regret. I wanted, so much, for you to say, You have my number, let's do this again.

But you just looked me square in the eye, said, Shut the door with force when you leave, the lock can be tricky.

I was sitting down with my end-of-shift bottle of helles, when your text flashed up on my phone. Forced myself to wait ten minutes before I opened the message, another seven before I permitted myself to respond. But playing it cool is a hopeless endeavour, particularly when we both knew I'd be round in no time. Apron away, tills emptied and locked, I retraced my steps to your place for the second time in under a day. Sweatier, dirtier and stinking of roasted cauliflower. I had tahini and tomato sauce stained into the cuffs of my shirt, and my hair was parted to the side by the day's grease. But the second visit was so much more tantalising . . . delicious, even – the pop of the bell, the buzz of the door, the soft thud of my feet on the stairs, and that creak of the door that you left ajar for me.

You stood there with your bloodshot eyes, high as a kite, a soft smile on your lips.

Na du . . . I thought you'd never make it.

Sorry, delays on the U8.

And then you led me by the hand and ate me out on the sofa, even though I said, I'm not sure if I'm clean.

Over time, the staff at work got used to the set-up; my phone vibrating on the bar while I necked the rest of my helles. What, is it already two? they'd ask with a wink and a laugh. Pass us your apron, go, skedaddle.

One night, you even texted at five – although I was long asleep, I found myself in admiration of that level of chutzpah.

Night after night, the same scene on repeat – a mess of limbs and digits on your mismatched bedding, red eyes and slurring, an overfilled ashtray carefully balanced between us. A side table cramped with a half-dozen bottles – poppers and beers and miniatures of whisky – and a DVD case shoved to the side with some perfectly formed lines of leftover weekend powder. And always a playlist on low, or an animated sitcom half watched in the background, because you were never one for fucking in silence.

And in those moments between – after sex, before sleep – we sat up talking about nothing of substance because you hated talking about anything 'too heavy' before bed. I learned that you have three brothers and a sister, and a best friend called Adel.

Why d'you keep asking about my friends and my family and my life at work? you asked.

I want to know who you are, what you do.

I told you already, you said.

But you hadn't. Not properly, not really.

Tell me again.

I identify software issues, put forward designs for new features – maintain the whole system. And then you reached for the joint and said, Can we change topic? Never one to mince your words.

In politics, we fared no better. The minute I started talking, you'd roll your eyes dismissively, slip your hand up my thigh and laugh as I ceased to speak coherently.

I asked you, What happened? How do you go from reading Memmi, Gibran and Darwish to silence?

Because none of it is important, you said. No need to dwell on the things that won't put money in your pocket.

I told you that's reductive, you don't really mean it.

Speak to me in five years, you said, let me know if you still feel the same.

You don't think politics, literature, art, are things worth discussing?

And you said, Depends where you are. If you're in parliament or a gallery, sure. But most of the time there's no point in it – who's actually listening? Returning to the laptop, you asked me if I had a preference – Arabic or electronic or that playlist we had on earlier?

Over time, the bookcase in your living room began to feel like a memorial to somebody else. I wanted to leaf through its books, see if it would surrender any clues, but I told myself, Leave it alone, no need to tamper with ghosts.

But you did engage once, do you remember? Early on, when I got us to watch that documentary on the West Bank settlements.

Said to you, I find it amazing how they always write out the Mizrahi presence.

And you said to me, You're too stuck in the details. Mizrahi, Ashkenazi . . . it's all complicity in occupation.

You called it an overindulgent conversation.

I said you can't understand the conflict without its internal divisions. Even the oppressed oppress. Who do you think carries out all the dirty work?

You said that from across the barrier, it must look like a fight between two captors over who got a bigger part of the loot.

And for the smallest part of a second, I got a glimpse into something close to an opinion. But then you ran your fingers along the ridge of my back and signalled to me the end of the chat.

After that, whenever you asked, What do you want to watch? I always returned the decision back to you, until it was no longer a question, but a ritual before streaming. And I was more than happy to zone out to your stoner comedies, particularly those Friday films you loved, starring Ice Cube and Tucker. I got a kick out of watching you laugh, a mouth crammed with food and a half-dozen styrofoam boxes opened before you – smoked aubergine and lamb skewers and lentils with rice – that I'd get the cooks at the back to quietly put aside.

But best of all, I liked it when the conversation turned to music, because then you had all the words in the world. Always an EP or an album to show me, or an obscure track you had recently discovered. And I would sit there listening to you speak, on just about any genre, from 80s ska and Sudanese funk to industrial techno (but never UK garage). You'd list off legendary parties and upcoming nights like the events page of Resident Advisor.

When I asked you what it was you liked so much about Berlin's clubs, you answered: Isn't that obvious?

Kinda, I said, but is it specifically the music? The drugs? The darkrooms?

You said, It's all that and more, and then you paused for a second.

It's the total freedom, you said at last. You can be whoever you want to be, for the night . . . for the weekend.

And I realised I was none the wiser as to who you really were, but I guess I didn't much care, not really, not nearly enough. I even deleted the app; though I was under no illusion to believe us exclusive, it was nice to put up my thumbs, rest them from all that scrolling.

*

I think the one time we left the confines of your bed was that time we went clubbing at Bergmann's Den. I texted you at the end of my shift, told you I was headed to the club with some of the restaurant staff.

Fifteenth anniversary, back-to-back weekend. Come?

I don't know.

It will be fun, I said, makes a change from hiding away in your duvet.

It was a big step, I know, thrusting us into public view like that. I told the rest of the staff to go ahead, that I was picking you up on the way. Sat waiting in the cab outside, wondering to myself if this counted as a first date.

We stood there in that queue decked out in our Sunday best – black vintage sportswear and string vests. You moaned about waiting, you peered this way and that, looking for a way to skip the queue. And once we were in, coats stashed away, spirits renewed, you slipped a quarter of a pill into my palm, ordered us a bottle of Coke, and told me to follow you to the back of the garden.

Fill the bottom of your mouth with Coke first, you said, and then you fed me G with a pipette. Got us so horny we fucked in the cold outside. And then afterwards as we sat by the main bit, where the door flapped open to spit out revellers and techno, with our legs all entangled, you told me, This *thing* is working out well. Those words lingered sweetly, but I was coming up fast, and I didn't have a way to properly say that I felt the same.

We moved into the sticky heat of inside, through the bodies packed tight on the dance floor, to a patch big enough for us to stand with our hands on our hips. The sun rose outside and the smoke machine filled the room, and we danced until we were covered in sweat. When we ran into the restaurant staff, I saw how they lapped up your smile, ate you up with their eyes – especially Dani and Yan (the white guys with the dark hair). I stood there beaming, as they signalled to me with their eyes: He's a cutie, Ronnie.

I couldn't hear what you'd shouted into their ears, but they seemed engaged and interested. And as they headed outside for some air, they squeezed my arms, and kissed me on both cheeks, like aunties wishing me mazal tov.

As soon as they left, you pressed on my tragus and spoke into my ear: Let's rack up a line. And then you grabbed hold of my hand and led me back out through a tunnel of torsos, lit cigarettes held like torches.

At the bathroom sink, as I filled up our bottles, I watched you embrace that guy with the harness and fan. Hugs and smiles, guarded and familiar, I listened to you switch between Arabic and German. When he left, you told me he was called Ziyad.

Sorry, you said, I should've introduced you. But he's in a bad place. Recently ended between him and some guy. I think he's been ghosted.

You think?

It's been three weeks, wala kilme.

Poor guy, that's shit. He probably hadn't seen it coming.

And you said, Of course he didn't. But these things happen . . . You know how it is.

I said that I did and that I blamed it on society, no one ever teaches us how to love another man.

And then you rolled your eyes, said, Just for tonight, no more politics. When I tried to protest you planted a kiss on my lips, and I stood there, silenced, content by the dryers, grinding my teeth.

The following evening, when we woke, and I disentangled myself from your warmth, made my way to work with my breath still sour, I felt that something between us had changed. And it wasn't just the effect of the pills. We had tiptoed over a line; you were no longer just a fuck buddy I saw after dark.

But two days passed, no word between us, and I left it alone because we needed the space to recover. But then four days passed, then five and six, and two texts and a call went unanswered.

I thought it strange that you should go for so long without answering, but perhaps something came up, there was probably a reason. I got fed up of checking my phone to see if you'd messaged, told myself, The ball is in his court, don't make any more effort.

Seven days turned to eight, and the unopened DMs began to pile. I kept checking for the little circular picture to appear underneath. And at work the only image that followed me all evening was two ticks left on read.

I started to agonise over every small detail. I overanalysed that night at the club and overthought every night that had preceded it. And every ambiguous sentence you'd said and every fleeting small moment we'd shared became grounds for a new interpretation that left me feeling more hurt.

Was it my politics? My topics of conversation? Had I done something to offend?

And on the phone, Dani said that it probably wasn't that. Some guys just get scared.

But I hadn't come on too strong. I never cornered you,

never asked you what to call us.

Still, Dani said, maybe he just felt trapped. And that's a personal thing to do with him, not a marker of what you had.

Trapped, how?

Maybe not trapped. Maybe scared. Maybe he just lost interest. And the thing is you won't know unless he says so. There's no point racking your brain, trying to find out what caused it to end. Do you want me to come round?

I told him no, that I needed to be alone, and hung up the phone.

I fought the urge to send you angry messages, kept them stored in drafts until the feeling passed.

Told myself, coming off crazy would help no one, particularly when I hadn't known you long enough.

Night after night, I sat there with my helles, waiting for my phone to vibrate. And the staff at the restaurant stopped making their jokes, and when they said go home, skedaddle, they did so after emptying the tips into the till, after I'd mixed up the bills, faces sour and pissed.

And the mornings all merged into one. I would just sit there all day in bed, smoking spliff after spliff, until my alarm went off at a quarter past five and reminded me to get ready for work. Every so often, Dani would check in, make me a cup of tea and an omelette in pita, and threaten to drop me off at the clinic Am Urban if I didn't start eating.

Look, Ronnie, it's shitty, he said, but life goes on. It's been three weeks. You can't continue to sit shiva. Go away for a week, somewhere good for your soul. Go and get yourself together again.

But where could I go?

Instead I just blocked you on WhatsApp, on Instagram, deleted your number from my phone.

Told myself that I was regaining control.

Your erasure became my self-preservation. I was no longer going to mourn for something so short-lived. I kept myself busy, took on extra shifts at work, yoga in the afternoons. I even cut out the joints.

Told myself, clear mind, clearer thoughts. I don't need to be smoking.

And when three weeks turned to four, I downloaded the app. Jockstraps and dick pics and terrible chat, all that bartering of goods at the market.

But with every guy I hooked up with, your rejection still returned to the surface. It sat like a hand on my throat, a balled fist pressed up to my belly. It took a while, maybe a month, or two, until I could have sex with a stranger without the fear of your rejection resurfacing.

None of those hook-ups left me with goosebumps. But I was OK with that, I didn't need more. I picked up guys in clubs, exchanged numbers in bars, stood waiting about in the shadows of darkrooms. And I even went out on dates, slowly clawing back my self-confidence.

Berlin is such a small place, and I often wonder if I'll see you again. I want it to happen, I think that it will, I've spent enough time imagining the scene. You're filling your bottle at the sink, techno in the background, your eyes wide and glazed, and then you spot me standing there by the dryers. Or you get on my carriage at Rathaus Neukölln, walk across and kiss me hello, and then you tell me that you've been so lost without me, could we please start over?

But other times, I envision a späti, and you're red-eyed and clutching one of those big packets of paprika crisps, and you seem genuinely excited to see me, but as I turn to leave, you say to your friend, Sorry, I should've introduced you, that was Ronnie, he's not in a good place.

It's all irrelevant anyway. I've met someone else. A yuppie from Holland who works for a start-up in Kreuzberg. He likes bio wines and Chinese food, and we fuck to *BoJack Horseman* on in the background. And, when I think of it, it was going so well, but I've left him on read three days in a row now.

And I guess this is a really roundabout way of saying, I've forgiven you Sami, even if you never said sorry.

Stolen

Ramya Jegatheesan

Listen.

Being a thief is no easy thing, hmm? It's a lightness in the ankles, a sharpness out the corner of your eyes, it's held breath, it's everything, OK-ma?

You can tell a lot about a person from what they steal. Never trust a boy – or girl – who steals kisses. If they steal one at the dead of night, under bridges, misjudged and misplaced, now be sure, you're better off without them. It's easy when you know, when you see the patterns. If somebody steals fruit, be sensitive. They will have lost someone in a war. Which war? World, Vietnam, Sri Lankan civil, any war, all wars – they kill you dead the same. Be kind, be tender, their heart will be bruised, smell fragrant, like a cut, red apple.

When someone steals something, look, look close-like. If you're smart, you'll know.

Me? The balls on you, asking about me! Barely know me still and asking deep deep questions. Well, well, I will respect your balls. I steal books. I steal bits of wall from crumbling ruins. I steal lipstick. Wound red, them all. I steal the white hair out your mass of black. Make of that what you will.

It's in my blood, see? My father used to work as an

accountant before he stole money from his boss. That was not his first infraction, though, because my mother said he stole the best years of her life. Said he stole the words right out her mouth, left her silent, mouldering, string-lipped. When I was a child, the sound of missing words was so oppressive, so choking, I'd run straight out of the house, into the arms of the palm trees that lined our plot of land. This was when we lived up north, in the village. Afterwards, when we moved to the city, running to a palm meant avoiding the crushing metal of cars. Not so good, no-yo.

So why did I pick up the family business if I knew the harm it left behind? Easy question, dumbo. Because there is a symmetry in thievery. I watched my father wither, too, the juice and marrow sucked right out his bones by what he gained. No other business has equality like that, no siree, not for a man the same as a woman. It is the only job where I lose and win the same as any moustachioed, swaggering, bighead-man. That is worth something something, no? Yes.

The first book I ever stole was *My Girl* by Margaret Mosby. I was working as a cleaner at the Omega Regency Hotel in Welawatte then, in the city down south. My aunt had got me the job, bless her tired, greying heart, wanting to help her one alive sister's pillai, help her girl-child stay out of trouble. And she knew that if I was underfoot, my father tripping over me, windmilling his psychic arms to stop his nose from smashing against the walls of my corner-eye cut looks, I'd definitely be in trouble. So she talked to her boss, got me a job and my job was to empty the bins in the oosh-pshh fancy rooms and replace the toilet rolls hanging next to the commode toilets. The first time I saw a commode toilet, I laughed. Who were these lazy-bumbums, who couldn't stretch their calves to squat, who thought that their kakaa needed to drop from a great height, so high high like birds, like their noses turned up. It was a good job, though, despite the bad porter. There were lots of things to steal. A whiff of expensive perfume in the air. A tinkle of laughter from a child playing. A moan turning to a pleaful murmur from one of the double rooms. The book, though, oh the book was the mael, the sweetest thing I stole that sumana, that month. I found it the day after some foreign tourists had left the room. I ask you, what would you have done-ma? Remember, there was no way of contacting them, no way of running after them in my itchy stockings the porter was always trying to put holes into, no return address in the book, none, nome, nothing, nope-nope. This was what I thought, hours later, when the book was already in my flat.

I can see what you're thinking, as clear as the skin on your face. This dark skin bad girl, Tamil-speaking terrorist black cat, shame to her family, shame to the fanny she plopped out of. Clasp your hand over your running mouth, nai, *listen*. Use your elephant-sized ears and *listen*. Bad girl or not, shame shame or not, I was clever. Straight scholarships to English medium schools, spoke three languages and a bit of some that didn't even exist anymore. I was smart, OK? And because I was smart, I knew that a career in thievery was the cleverest thing I could do.

I had other jobs too, seriya, because art doesn't pay much, not even where I'm from. Especially where I'm from. And stealing is an art – you listen to me when I say that, acca, it is. After the hotel job (I was let go when the porter was found on top of me, trying to stuff me into him and him into me), there were other good jobs. But it's the stealing I remember, clear clear. For two days a week, I stole someone's identity. It was blissful, like scratching a mosquito bite, that good feel where your eyes roll into the back of your head. Except I don't scratch mosquito bites no more, not after my seventeenth cousin, Kunju, told me scratching the bites gave you dengue, and she should really know, her brother dying in the hospital from the fever. Not even the doctors could do anything. Imagine that.

Those were the good days. I stole another book from the rebuilt Jaffna Library when I went back up north to visit family. Turning up during tourist hours, I was pretty much alone. The hush hush is the same in libraries the world over – no, no, I tell a lie. There was one library in London, so loud, I'm not sure it was a library. I didn't even steal anything from there, so discombobulated I was from the speaking and the singing. Weird weird place. But Jaffna Library, you could wear the quiet like a blanket, like the blankets the tea-plantation workers wear in the Upcountry, itchy itchy cloth to keep the bitey bitey cold out. The library was not cold, though. I can see my veiny feet plodding barefoot on the dried-blood marble floor. Can't you? Pay attention, then. I don't speak for my health, you know. It was warm in the library, humid, the sweaty embrace of an aunty you love. I missed that heat, I did. The air conditioning in the city left me cold, shivery, making me think I was frightened when I was *not*. I missed the geckos of the north, their prolificacy, their profundity. They were around in Colombo too, but they were always shooed off, shooed away. There was no time to admire their bulbous eyes, their thin skin, the dark blots of their stomach and heart, beating, beating. Maybe it was a good thing, though. I was always afraid in Colombo that someone would see a pali and slap it smushed. On purpose, by accident, it wouldn't matter, no. Dead is still dead.

Oh, what did I steal? Easy, acca, easy. Let me tell it my way, who do you think you are? Tssk. I stole a browning copy of *Gone With the Wind*. It was thick and good, but I stole it for the cover, I think. Ooofa, the mangos on the lady on the front! Lurid, lurid stuff. It made me laugh. Also, it didn't smell like smoke. All the other books – the palm-leaf manuscripts, the old cloth-bound tomes – they all smelt like smoke. These books weren't around during the fire, the librarian told me when I asked. Then why the smell like smoke, you tell me? If they weren't here when people burned and my people's history burned, why do they smell like smoke? No answer now, eh, dancing mouth? I stole the book for reasons I can't be bothered to remember. Maybe I just liked books by Margarets.

What do you mean, get to the story? This is the story, dumb-dumb. This is all the story if you listen. The fact that the library followed no earthly realm of categorisation is the story, the fact that I wasn't there when my father died is the story, the fact that *you* asked *me* for the story, is the story. Clasp your hands together. What's inside them? That's the story.

You smile. Good. You have strong teeth. My first ever boyfriend had teeth like pearls. There was no unnatural glimmer, but they shone strong and white in the night. When he smiled, I could find his mouth like a lighthouse, draw near to a kiss like a moth.

I stole my first ever bit of history at Jaffna Fort. Listen, I wasn't the first to steal there and I won't be the last. Unpucker that gooseberry mouth of yours and ask, Who stole

91

it first? The land it's built on, the smashed-up temples, the Portuguese took to build their fort. Then the Dutch came and slapped it out their hands. Then the British came, and it was given meekly, stolen like taxes. Then it was relinquished to Ceylon, with the bad humour independence brings, and then the LTTE took it when they wanted it and then the Sri Lankan army yanked it back. Neighbouring villagers stole chunks of masonry to fix the holes the war had left in their homes. The fort is a laundry list of thievery, why begrudge me my little piece of coral brick? I had just wanted to visit. I had just wanted to see. They had plundered the ocean to build the fort, you realise, building the walls and floors with coral stone. Why do you blame me for looking at the ramparts with their stripes and striations, the circular starbursts and meandering lines like brains, and wanting? God, I wanted so bad. Every day is a wanting. Do you never feel it? The fome? That there is a want in your blood, in your stomach, behind your eyes, in the palm of your tongue, in the purse of your lungs – do you not want so much that it makes you laugh and cry? Don't look at me like that. Go away, go, if you can't do anything but look at me that way. Glinty glinty eyes do not empathy make. I wanted a part of that fort, so I took it. Stood on the bastion facing the sea, with a bit of coral in my hand. This was yours, I wanted to yell at the sea and raise my fist. They mined the waves to build its watcher, I thought. The fort looks over what made it, so cautious-like, so wary-like. I kept thinking the fort would move, like a turtle shaking off the earth after winter, and slowly, inexorably, paddle its way out to sea. What of me, then, eh? What would I do in the sea? Very bloody little.

I went to see the hanging platform. How did I know it was once a hanging platform? I don't know, I just knew. I'm clever, I told you. Dropped the facts in your ear but it's an empty tunnel up there, so it fell out the other way, didn't it? Don't shake your head too hard. Maybe something will stick if you sit still.

I just knew, tsch. I knew. My feet told me this was where people were hanged until they died. Looking out to sea. But who am I kidding, do you think the vellakaran would have let them see the ocean just before they died? No, no. I bet they put a bag over those bowed, dark-slick heads. They would want their last sight to be of blankness, the smell of their own terrified breath. I am not a thief like them. I do not steal like they once stole. Why should I be punished for crimes less severe than theirs?

Ah, you are paying attention. Yah, I *am* deflecting, procrastinating, delaying, deferring, postponing – *whaat*? Enna? Child born to a buffalo, what do you want now? Enna VENNAM? Oh-Kaaii.

Won't let a woman tell a story in her own time. The world we've come to.

I walked to the hanging platform, what which I knew was a hanging platform because I am a genius. The platform looked out to sea and the sea looked blandly back. I realised there was a couple tucked against one of the four pillars that held the roof up, shaded by that wooden canopy. The woman, her hand on his chest, leaning into his body, her feet between the square of his. Looking up into his face. The wind blew in the salt off the sea and then like magic, the view in front of me dropped its veils and I saw. My boyfriend, standing there, looking down at the girl, his teeth shining. She looked like me. That's all I could say for days after, whispering into my pillow, my hair, the corners of whatever room I had to be in.

She looked like me. I watched them for a while. In my head, I saw the girl being swiped across the scene, swipe, swipe, swipe. Each swipe revealed a new girl, looking up at my boyfriend with what I could imagine was a sweet tenderness, like the inside of a rambutan on your lips. Swipe, swipe. Them all looking the same, thin and narrow-wristed, narrow-necked, swinging on a loop of his smile. Swipe.

At home, I realised I had gripped my stolen bit of coral so hard, there were imprints on my palm. It changed my palm lines, you know. Had to go get another reading, now that the first one was defunct. The old man looked at my new lines, raised white caterpillar eyebrows and sighed.

Aiyo, he said, but softly. No need to call Death to your door with his wife's name. He said it quiet-like. Aiyoo.

When my phone stopped ringing with my boyfriend's calls, when his wet-ass, sorry excuses stopped taking up my storage, I went to Cargills Food City in Jaffna town and stole lipstick. It was red and matte and slid on like mist. It was a fancy-pancy place, the Food City, a bit oosh-pshh, built for vacationing members of the diaspora whose children grew sick of rice and curry after a few days, and for aspirational townies. Practise foreignness on pasta sauces that cost more than a day's wage before you leave to go London or Canada or Germany or Australia or wherever gleamed bright for that generation's export of young, shiny minds. It was a good lipstick. I shook my cousin upside down for ages when she used it to apply one, round, perfect pottu on the middle of her forehead.

Not yours, not yours, I said, shaking her until her tears made a little pool for ants. Secretly, though, I was proud. Getting into the family business. I rewarded her with slices of cool apple, later. That cousin isn't here anymore. The whole family moved away. I mean I did too, but I always came back. She didn't. I wonder if she kept up the family trade.

Hmm? No, I don't. Hmm? Oh, well. I stole for the wanting, you see-ma. Acca, that's all I ever stole for. Anna, listen, I promise. The last time I was home, Amma was sick in her bed. I wanted to buy her a mattress, but she said it was too high off the floor. A mat on the floor was all she wanted. I wanted her further away from the ground, but she wouldn't listen. Donkey-like, the stubbornness I learnt from her. I held her hand. I wanted to unstitch her mouth, make her tell me everything. I wanted her to give her words to me. No thievery in her last moments, no stealing from my amma. I put my head on her shoulder and willed her heart to tell me anything she wanted. I would listen to it all. *You shamed me, you let me down, make me tea, I'll make you tea, I'm happy I'll see my brother again, I'm worried I'll see your father again –* anything, everything. I would have collected her words and strung them together like the brightest, saddest jewellery out there, wear it down my hair part, around my waist, around my ankles, wear it how only our people did, wear something no one could steal from me. She didn't say anything. When she died, I wasn't sure I'd done the right thing. She didn't need it all where she was going. But I did. I was alone now. I needed it, something, anything, but she took it away with her. I should have been a thief.

Yes.

So there – there. You have it, now. Got what you wanted. That's what you wanted, enna? Stolen from me. You know that, right? Stolen from me. I wonder what it weighs on you.

I wonder what it lifts from me. Clasping my hand, what foreignness is this? We don't shake hands here. Keep them to yourself.

No, you did steal it. I did not give it to you. I am no fool. The having is in the thievery.

Go, now. Yes. You have it now. Go.

Go.

The Spot

Aden Jamal

Abdi, your dads here. He doesnt know when he goes back

This was my half-sister's text, but they were her mother's words, my father's second wife's words, I could tell.

He had been missing three days now. I'd stopped washing my school uniform every couple of days – the chalky, perfumed washing powder was low. The fresh food was gone. The rice and spices had run out and I had a hunger that I was familiar with hating. All my childhood, I'd never been comfortable enough to believe that my hunger wouldn't return. It was as frequent and unwelcome as the rain on this island. The flat held the cold, dim grey light of emptiness as, stomach growling, burning, I locked my phone and shrugged on my school blazer.

We went to the fried chicken takeaway for lunch. We called it the chicken spot, the spot; I can't remember why. I didn't get free school meals anymore, my father couldn't be bothered signing the three or four forms for me to eat, so I wound my hour cotching away from the school canteen, in the spot on the High Street with Eddie and Ains. Today, that smell of dirty delicious chicken that this city lies in, the salt and the fat, the dense odour of steaming flesh, was more shameful to me. It felt extravagant, extra and heavy; I didn't deserve to sit there, starving in the thick stench.

'Yo – take a chip.' Ains brandished his paper bag, greasy, but with the scratchy sound of crisp chips rubbing against too much salt.

Ains was always sharp. He could see I was hungry but lacked the sense to ask me why. Instead, he wanted to ease it. While Eddie, done with his bones and down to just soggy leftovers, was busy wasting time and energy needlessly mashing his last few chips, ketchup and all, into a pulpy, bloody mess.

I dropped a chip, salty, oily, crisp, into my desperate mouth. There was so much saliva that I thought my mouth might overflow, that the chip might sog away into nothing, into a memory of contentedness that left me looking like a freak with drool foolishly hanging from my tongue in ropes. A few grains of salt worked their way onto my cracked lips, caustically burning in my pleasure. I tried to disguise my hungering face, but I was sure I failed.

A man stood at the end of the long counter, leaning lazily in a tight white T-shirt and baggy tracksuit bottoms. He was staring straight at me and had the same look that I had – hungry, starving, needful. His stare stripped my guard. I sensed that, like some teachers or Ains's mother, he saw straight to the desperate boy that I was.

His arms were huge, bigger than my legs, bigger than any arms I had ever seen that weren't on TV or in pornos online. They bulged under his T-shirt with a life of their own. Worlds away from the lazy, fatty arms of my father, this man's elephantine arms were for a different purpose. He continued to stare at me as I looked away, cowed. I felt danger in that corner. And that to look at him would be an invitation. The opposite was true.

He talked to the server, cutting in front of all the kids waiting for their cheap lunches, and came to our table with a burger, two pieces and some fries. He put the tray in front of me and sat down opposite, blocking Eddie from leaving.

'Eh, you're starvin' init? Eat, man.'

I didn't say anything. Eddie immediately stopped mashing his chips, as though he'd been caught by his mum, and looked down at his hands. But it was Ains that warned me. Ains shook next to me – I felt it through the plastic chairs, cheap hard things connected by a thin metal bar. Ains was afraid of nothing. Not his three older, bigger brothers. Not his mother, just shy of six feet, angry as acid – he took right after her. He wasn't even afraid of the head teacher, Mr Elliot, who he'd flung a shaving-foam bomb at on the last day of term last year. This Ains, like a dog in front of a bear, shook and shrank. This Ains was alien to me. But I *was* starving. What could I do . . . ?

There was a hush in the shop – even the two Asian men behind the counter stopped throwing fries into the scalding oil to bloom so they could watch what I would do.

All entrepreneurs spot their opportunities. And they exploit them ruthlessly. They are parasites. And drug dealers are the biggest parasites, the biggest entrepreneurs, in the world. My hunger, my dirty mouth, my cracked and desperate fingers moved independently and tore the chicken, broke the chips to splinters, ground the burger to mush; I ate and ate and ate shamelessly.

'Come to me, yea? Next time you're hungry. I'm here,

I'll be here when you are. And they'll sort you out with some chicken or kebab if I'm off,' the man said, nodding at the guys behind the counter, who seemed to hear and pretend they didn't hear at the same time – or maybe they just understood the opportunity, from experience. Standing up with a jangle, the man, ignoring Eddie completely but eyes lingering on Ains with a hostility that I sensed rather than saw, left the shop. And he left me full and dazed.

Overnight – as my belly ached and burned, writhing within me like a bloated snake, a mind of its own, reminding me of my hunger, reminding me I'd had no dinner or breakfast, reminding me I was killing myself – I thought desperately of the chicken spot. The salt, the thick taste of golden brown, soothing away my burning hunger. It tormented my night, the memory, kept my eyes open, slipped into my agonising dreams like a knife, holding my rest ransom.

The next morning, as I dressed my protesting belly, I thought only of the chicken spot. My bag, with yesterday's books, lay ignored. My school uniform, splattered with ketchup and grease from yesterday's one binge, went on again – despite the staring eyes I'd attract, the barely held-back laughs in the school corridors. The teachers would scold me for forgetting my books, they'd tell me off for not paying attention, send me out of the classroom for not trying, but it didn't matter. Lunchtime was all that mattered.

'Where'd you go? You ran straight from maths,' Eddie whispered, while Mrs Chalmers explained, for the twelfth time, the difference between a simile and a metaphor to the sleepy low set boys and girls. 'Did you skip it and get some food?'

The man's name was Jamal, I'd found out. He owned the spot – he owned the chicken he fed me. The memory of his face loomed over me as I thought back to my long lunch ten minutes ago, just before English. Ains and Eddie hadn't come but I'd eaten enough for them both. I thought of Jamal telling me about his dad, about how his dad had left and never come back. About how his mother had also died young. About having to eat, no matter what. I didn't repeat any of this to Eddie – there was something shared between me and Jamal now, some rope or chain we both understood, held together.

English, like maths, like science, placed me and Eddie away from Ains. A scrunched-paper ball flew happily across the room as soon as Mrs Chalmers turned her back to start scribbling on the board. A three-hundred-page book, *The Merchant of Venice*, which may have been written in French for all I knew, was flung in response.

The heavy splatter of pages against the wall to Eddie's left caught Mrs Chalmers' attention.

'Year Eleven!' she barked. We wore smirks and lip curls – we were used to her pointless scolding by now. 'Your exams are in *two months*! I do not expect to have to spend every few minutes turning around to make sure that you aren't killing each other! You are all sitting the foundation paper, so you need to pay extra attention – especially you boys at the back!' she said, training her gaze, as ever, on the four dark, most disruptive boys in the shadowy corner of the room, with their fades, braids and AF1s. 'You should all be ashamed that not one of you can tell me what a metaphor is. Now focus!' she finished, a hint of begging in her high-pitched timbre. As she turned to the board, a chair, empty, plastic, heavy, worthless, flew across the room like a missile, smashing into the bookcase at the front of the class. Jake, attention-starved, tie off, around his head inexplicably, cried out in triumph. 'The chair's a metaphor!' he shouted, jumping onto the table and whooping.

'GET OUT!' Mrs Chalmers streaked across to Jake's seat as he ran along the tables like a beast.

'Ains was wondering where you got to,' Eddie told me, louder now that Jake's distraction held the whole class in its madness, and the conversations that had been paused were momentarily restarted.

'I got lunch, init – what does it matter?'

'He thought you'd gone back to the spot, you know?'

'It's none of your fucking business,' I said, surprising myself with my ferocity. 'And where were you guys anyway? Do you see me botherin' you?'

I must have surprised Eddie, too, who hesitated, then went silent. The April sky outside, turbulent, cast shadows and gentle light across the classroom walls.

'He's . . . he's scared, init. He's scared of that guy.'

'He's a pussy, then,' I said, not believing myself.

'Oi, bruv! Look, look at Abdi's shirt!' Keith burst into theatrics, pointing at my clothes. 'Dutty pum pum juice yu nah! Ha ha ha!'

I felt an instant burn of anger. I thought of Jamal's arms, of how I wanted them to squeeze Keith's throat.

'It's ketchup,' Eddie shouted, going from two to ten in an instant, picking up his own copy of *The Merchant of Venice* to throw.

'RIGHT,' burst out Mrs Chalmers savagely, finally ejecting Jake from the classroom, who would now wander the halls spectrally till drama. 'SIT DOWN, EDDIE! SILENCE!

Back to today's lesson,' she insisted, buying herself half a moment's respite.

A jet-engine rumble greeted me as I left the school gates that afternoon. It came from a black Mercedes parked across the road, windows tinted aggressively, so that only the pale reflections of school uniforms turned in desperation, in wonder, could be seen. Music blared, thumping bass tones shattering the air, the pavements, shattering and claiming that imperceptible space in our unconsciousness. It was a firework tossed into the heaving masses of our everyday school routine, drawing the eyes of every pupil walking alongside me, of every teacher stood at the gates in security, shepherding us frantically away at the close of another school day, back into the concrete fields of London. There was another jet-engine rev and, window rolling down, Jamal's lazy mid-tone arm popped out and beckoned to me. I walked shyly over, heart beating a dull rhythm.

'Yo, get in, bruv,' he said, as a metallic *click* cut through the bass. I hesitated, sensing the eyes of the hundreds on me, sweating slightly under my stinking blazer, imagining my thick stench of BO and fried chicken pervading the car air. But I had never before been in such a big, sleek car – I'd only ever been in the clapped-out VWs of a few distant cousins, and once in a rented white van, suspension so jumpy I'd skinned my knee on the dashboard. I clumsily fell into the back seat, slowly shutting the door behind me.

The bass was heavy. The music shaking my skin and bone with its selfish need. The seats, soft and warm in the April sun, so firm that I thought I was sat on a new mattress in a store, felt like an unreal comfort. Finally looking up, I saw with a start that beside Jamal was a woman.

'Hi!' she said with an authoritative smile. 'I'm Jaime – Jamal's told me all about you!' She licked her lips slightly. Her accent, a southern cheeriness, disarming, had an edge to it that matched the powerful, sleek car and tight ponytail, that told me to stay on her good side. I kept my eyes on her.

'Aww, your smile is so nice – you should smile more, such big dimples! Shouldn't he smile more, babe?' Jamal stayed silent, watching the schoolboys and girls, watching the teachers. 'Bet the girls all love you . . . I would have!' she added, turning away. Jamal kissed his teeth. 'Jaime, shush,' he hissed, revving the engine. Jaime, eyes so soft, quickly sharpened her gaze onto Jamal.

The car engine, throbbing, thrust us forward into the empty street with a rumble that encased me, that violated me, that seemed to lift and crush and stretch me all at once. The force of Jamal's foot on the pedal pushed me further back, into the leather sea.

'Yo, I'm taking you to shops, bruv. You can't be eating no more chicken for your food init. You'll be sick.'

'And we're getting you some new, nice, trainers, aren't we?' Jaime asked, serenely. When Jamal said nothing, she continued, 'And a new shirt, I think.'

I hadn't thought to ask where we would be heading. It surprised me, how easily I'd gotten in and allowed myself to be driven off. To be taken care of.

At the clothing store, Jamal stayed on his phone while Jaime helped me try on shoes. She recommended the whitest pair of AF1s I'd ever seen, showing off her matching, white, pristine, perfect pair, walking comfortably in her skin-tight tracksuit, ponytail swaying. Jamal, walking outside to make a call, gave me a look as he dialled. A brief, odd look. A hungry, starving look. It confused me – how could he, with his Mercedes, with his chicken shop, with Jaime, hunger for anything?

'He's nice,' Jaime told me, watching Jamal pace outside. 'I'm glad he found you, he's one of the nicer ones I've been with.'

I didn't ask what she meant, walking backwards and forwards in my new shoes that sharply pinched the sides of my toes, stabbing with every step as though I'd already walked for miles in them. I didn't dare tell her how they felt; I didn't want her sharp gaze.

At the supermarket I was in heaven, in ecstasy. We pushed one of the big trolleys, the kind I'd only ever used before Christmas or bank holidays, and I was allowed whatever I wanted. I shovelled in box after box of cereal, large bags of frozen chips, frozen pizzas, frozen burgers, more beans than I would ever have been able to carry. I bought sweets and crisps and four multi-packs of Coke cans. I wasn't sure how much I could get away with, and only slowed down when Jaime, with her smile dropping and dropping, asked the air: 'Shouldn't we get, like, some fruit or something?'

'Nah, let the yout' go!' Jamal said, sniggering as he picked up a box of coco pops, laughing at the monkey on the box before dropping it back into the trolley. 'You done though, init?' he said, not really as a question, more as a warning. He looked down the aisles, watching and watching, always watching for something.

'We gotta get the drinks for tonight though, remember?' Jaime quickly said to Jamal, running down to the alcohol aisle.

'Nah, J, later init,' shouted Jamal after her. 'We'll get it later!'

She ignored him and continued, trying to turn the corner into the alcohol aisle. At the same moment, a trolley, one of the other shoppers not watching, came from the aisle and bumped into Jaime's hip. It wasn't a hard hit, making a soft bump into her pink tracksuit bottoms, but it was enough to stop her, to make her gasp in shock and knock a bottle of red wine from a shelf to smash, solitary, loudly, onto the dirty, unyielding tiles.

'Oh, I'm sorry!' came a cultured, soft, drawl. The sudden silence of the store held us all. Jamal, always watchful, always ready, started to move at a colossal speed, like a stalking beast, heavy and unstoppable, eager for the fight. It was an aggressive and frightening movement that I'd not seen from him.

'WHAT THE FUCK, MAN! WHAT YOU DOIN'?' Jaime screamed, shrieking and waving her fingers. 'You could have fucking run me ova', you batty man!' The silence was slashed, and all eyes turned, captivated by the outburst.

'I'm sorry,' the voice begged, shivering, alone in the cold aisle. Moving to the left I could see the man, short, balding, looking at Jaime desperately, begging with his eyes now for this to stop, to be allowed to leave, to sink into the floor. 'I'm sorry, I wasn't looki–'

'LOOK AT MY FUCKING CREPS!' she exploded, finally spotting the red wine, splattered like blood across her formerly white, perfect trainers. Her eyes, too, were red, her lips spitting; she was formidable and so different with her edge exposed to the world. Jamal, dragging her, pushed her towards me before turning round to settle it.

'*You bald cunt,*' he uttered, his voice low and dangerous. A voice I'd not heard from him, a voice that crawled like venomous spiders, that slithered into my ears. We all saw his hand slip into his tracksuit pocket and grasp something solid, twist it in the man's direction under the cloth. 'Watch when I catch you outside. *Watch for me.*'

The man, shaking now, stood transfixed in Jamal's gaze. It seemed to take an age before something snapped and the man, moving suddenly, moving quickly, scuttled to the exit, leaving his bursting trolley, yeast and flour and chutney and wines, abandoned. Jaime, still shouting, was held back now by the invisible force that was Jamal's malevolence ahead of us, between us and the man.

I looked beyond her. And saw Ains, scrawny, shocked, standing behind a trolley next to the giant sacks of basmati rice, watching us. It was as if someone had transported my former self here to view me. My chest sank to my knees and I shuddered, spotting his mother next to him, watching us, a fearless disappointment etching her frown lines, her wrinkled face, as she burned herself into me.

'So '*dis* your company now, eh?' she asked me, her thick Grenadian accent carrying through the aisles, ringing over the commotion. The other shoppers, confused by this woman now entering the fray, turned to look in the direction of her gaze. I felt torn, pained. Ains's mother had known me for years, had always been kind to me, even as she'd scolded me and Ains: for being silly; for wanting what the other boys our age wanted; for not working hard enough; for working too hard. She had always fed me, when I'd come round to cotch with Ains. But I hadn't been round too much lately. The gap between us, between our schoolwork, our trajectories, between our aspirations and disillusions, had grown over the years. But she was always kind, even when I couldn't be, even when I couldn't let Ains stay over, couldn't feed him in return. Even as I never invited them round to meet my family, my father. She had probably been the closest, over the years, to a mother. Not because we were close, and not because she was particularly mothering, but because there was nothing else for me – no friendly, nurturing female figure. She had given me a drop, a small, sweet-and-sour taste of what I lacked.

'Do you know this *woman*?' Jaime asked me, not unthreateningly, but slightly warily.

'I know *you*,' Ains's mother spat. 'And 'im,' she continued, pointing. 'I know exactly who you are. What you do.'

'What? Who you think you are? You can't tell me shit, you and your dickhead son always *interferin'*. At school tryin' ta tell me what I can do, what I can move. Shut your mout'.'

Ains's mother gave Jamal and Jaime the dirtiest, filthiest look she could, a look that almost withered the food in my trolley, and then she turned herself round. But not before turning that same look onto me. I shrivelled under it, ashamed, under the lights of the store. I clung tighter to the trolley, looking down at the playful monkey on the cereal box laughing up at me, belly so round, so full, like I wanted.

* * * * *

'It's his mum's fault,' I cried out, angry for once. I usually kept a firm hand on myself – as a child, I'd always sensed the disappointment from my father for being too emotional;

emotion was to him a crutch that good Somali men were not allowed. It was the evening of the next day and I was back at the chicken spot. 'They wouldn't let me out for lunch. I had to stay after school, too. They saw me get in your car. They want to know who you are, what's going on. She told the school about the shops. They said it was "just till they could speak to my dad". They want him to straigh'en it out. It's her, tellin' stories.'

As I moaned, Jamal seemed to find it funny. He showed no anger, now that it was only us two. He just chuckled. It was comfortable.

'Her, man. She's a twat,' Jamal said easily. Whenever he swore, it was as though he wasn't swearing, as though the words were just a regular part of his speech, not nettles in the field ready to itch. 'She used to try tell me e'ryday to do what she said, to stop botherin' her boys, the other boys.' Jamal cast his eyes across the room. 'Her son used to be my boy. But she *loved* interferin', poking her fat gob in. Forget her, forget her dumb son.'

'But the school . . .' I said, still nervous about their attempts to call my dad. About what would happen if the phone kept on ringing. How long before they got suspicious? Before someone was sent to my house?

'Nah, don't worry 'bout that. You got your keys, yeah?'

I pulled out my set, embarrassed a little by the fuzzy keyring I still kept, a little green frog Ains had thrown at me once upon a time. Jamal snatched them up before I could think about it.

'I'll sort it,' he said. 'I'll call them from your house, so they can see the number, and pretend to be your dad – his accent's thick, yeah? They won't question it . . . Warya! Haa?'

he finished, in a plastic, passable accent. I laughed, despite myself, at his surprisingly plausible Somali voice. 'They won't say nuthin' – they won't want to be called racist or some shit.

'Listen, I got something for you.' Reaching into his pocket he pulled out cards, cash, papers, all in a stack. No wallet, it was all just sat in his tracksuit pocket in a pile. He teased out two fifty notes, five twenties and a deck of train tickets, flicking through a few of the orange slips before he found the right one. He gave me the money first – the fifties, thick, unused, pristine and glowing warm as embers, were something I had never seen before. They transfixed me. I grinned as he gestured at me to put them in my pocket.

'I've got a job for you, yeah? Do it and there'll be more – think how much coco pops you can get with that!' Jamal joked. I laughed but Jamal, joke already over, looked around the empty shop. It was just before the evening rush, the commuters outside walking home, an hour or two before dinner.

'There's a bag, some stuff I got. I need you to take it for me and give it to a friend of mine who's waiting. That's all you gotta do, yeah? Just take this bag and give it to him. I told him you're coming, to look for you, what you look like. Then come straight back, back here. You'll be back in time for some food init, won't take too long. That's it. Sound good?'

Opposite him in the booth I nodded, not really thinking. All I could do was nod. It seemed simple; stacked up against everything Jamal had given me, this was a tiny favour, a thank-you card against a monstrous gift. He would pay me. He would clear up the school stuff so I could get lunch. I needed that, more than the money really. My father had

110

already been away for a week. I felt the shadow over me of what might happen if they found out.

'Good. The place is Stroud. That's where you need to go . . .'

Stroud. Seemed a strange word, a strange place. I had no clue where it was, what direction, how far. I knew nothing beyond London, nothing about this country.

'It's not far, yeah, like an hour and a half, man, *at most*. You'll be back here for dinner, I'll take you somewhere nice, proper chicken init, peri peri or some shit.' I shrugged, nodded. 'And my boy will be at the station, yeah? Right there. You won't even have to leave the station that much. Here's your ticket. It's two singles so you need to move now, you can't miss the train, yeah?' The low, dangerous voice from the supermarket was back, this time trained on me, suddenly and confusingly, so that I felt like a spotlight had clicked onto me, was dazzling me. Jamal looked straight at me. My heart beat a complex rhythm as I met his gaze, fearful but, I realised, more scared of failing, of letting him down. There was a glow about him that drew me, drew the starved, starving child in me.

'Remember how much I've given you, yeah? But also, what I'm gonna give you,' he continued, voice gentler. He glanced around the room again to make sure we were alone, just the two servers behind the counter; one, slowly easing, teasing thick, soft mayonnaise from one bottle into another; the other, throwing meat into the hot oil, to blister and curl and burn. 'I've done you some favours, but it's cool init, this is easy – just don't be late, drop the bag off and come back. My boy will know you, he'll find you, just wait at the entrance to the station, yeah? And when you get back . . .' Jamal reached

111

into his tracksuit again '. . . you'll have one of these.' He looked around once more, to be sure we were still alone, and flicked out a pen knife, long, shiny and glittering with a menace of possibility that reminded me of the metalwork pieces we used to make in DT, that reminded me of the solid structure, the form not yet taken, that I would see coming together before my eyes as I bent the metal into shape.

Paddington Station was empty space, airy and exposed. It was dinner time. I would usually be ignoring the chore of homework now and was relieved to not be worrying about being shouted at for forgetting to finish my bus stop division, even as I felt the black canvas straps from the holdall Jamal had handed me bind my back and shoulders.

The holdall was heavy, unexpectedly so given how soft it looked. I was afraid to open the zip, even the tiniest bit. I knew that Jamal couldn't possibly have eyes on me; I was no longer a child, but some childish fear remained. I still knew that this was a test, I still believed that he would know magically if I opened the bag. And I couldn't fail him – I didn't want to, I was realising.

There were few people in the station – one or two suited, the odd family or couple, some railway workers; but mostly it was deserted. The commuters were home. The students long gone. There was a patch of officers patrolling. One, bearded, tall, looked at my school uniform curiously . . . but then, bored, he allowed his eyes to glaze and shift away from me.

I thought of the text Jamal had just sent: *If your asked then say your seeing your brother at uni init, they won't say shit man*

The train, huge, wide, with swinging slow doors that I

had to coax open myself, so unlike the regimented, controlled Underground trains that I was used to, was a wilder, alien world. The carriages, empty, so much space, teased me. But they stared back at me too. Lonely, tragic. I looked down at my new creps in the vacuum, my gift from Jamal and Jaime. They pinched me, hard, at the sides of both my feet. With every step. I wouldn't ever tell Jamal. I'd rather lose my toes than admit it. But they tore at my feet every second, like hidden bear traps, biting me, making each step a labour. I sat down gratefully, relieved to get moving.

I noticed, as I double-checked my ticket, a minuscule red spot on my hand. It looked like red sauce, but darker . . . I wasn't sure if it was from lunch, or from the fifty notes, or the knife I'd briefly touched, or maybe the bag . . . but I didn't want to touch it or lick it to find out. Spitting slightly, I rubbed the spot using the orange train ticket, colours mixing into a swirl of partnership, forming something new, red sweeping into the ticket's gritty orange.

Tapestry

Aisha Phoenix

Loom woke on the morning of her fourteenth birthday feeling exactly the same as she had the day before. She had convinced herself that The Change would come. Like so many girls before her, she would be stuffed full of tiny sweet cakes and juicy sugar fruit, and given glasses of wild-grass juice to drink. She would be carried down to the Tapestry on the donkey that belonged to Mother Yemi, the leader of the village women, and her destiny would be decided. She was born to be a storyteller. Soon everyone would know that was what she was.

She rose early and went outside the small, tin-roof wooden cabin she shared with her mother to watch the firebirds drink nectar from the crimson flowers of the flame tree.

'Hear me and I shall tell it,' Loom said, and she began rehearsing her story of how the firebirds came to the island. She waved her arms, whispered and shouted to give life to her words. When she became a storyteller, she would be paid handsomely to tell such stories. There would be invitations to mark special occasions, and sponsorship from the wealthiest families on the island.

By the time she set off down Nest Hill, she was already

running late for school. Her path was flanked by nest trees with thick, interweaving roots until she arrived at the wooden cabins where her friends, Tress and Taya, lived with their mothers. Loom abandoned the path and half ran, half slid down the side of the hill through lizard ferns that reached up to her waist. She rejoined the path where the ground levelled out, catching up with Tress and Taya.

To her right was Little Boat Harbour and the sea that stretched to the horizon. Braid, her mother, would be out catching ocean seed. As she and her friends made their way up the hill to their dusty white school with its rusty tin roof, she told them the story of the firebirds, which made their eyes widen with wonder.

While Mister Thomas wrote equations on the board, she scrawled stories in her exercise book, only turning to maths when he began prowling between the rows of desks.

When Loom returned home, Braid showed her the silverfin she'd saved for her from the day's catch. That was the only thing that made the day different from any other. After supper they sat together on the step under a lantern and her mother helped her with her maths. Loom hated equations, but they delighted her mother more than words.

Three weeks later The Change came – sticky brown, then red. It was her fallow day, the day she tended the earth seed, the hairy brown-skinned milk fruit and the small knobbly moon potatoes they cultivated on the patch of land behind their home. Usually, when she finished, she would go down to Black Sand to tell Tress and Taya stories and play in the waves. Today she ran barefoot down to Little Boat and stood in the shadow of the gnarled knowledge tree, waiting for

Braid to return with the catch. She helped the women haul in the shimmering ocean seed, and watched as her mother calculated in her head how many fish to give to each of the women, dividing the catch according to the size of their family and the number of days they had each worked. The rest would be sold in the market and the profits shared according to Braid's formula.

When her mother had finished, Loom leaned in close and said, 'The Change has come.'

Her mother pocketed the knife she was holding, wiped her hands on her overalls, and gave Loom a hug. Then she took off her headscarf, releasing her colourful yarn-woven plaits, and tied the heavy cloth over her daughter's afro. 'It's come,' she said to the other women, with a slight nod of her head.

The women clacked their wellies together in a show of respect, and as Loom passed by, they touched her headscarf and offered blessings. Braid held her hand, which she hadn't done for years, and led her back up the hill to their home. For once, Loom sat while Braid fetched buckets of water to fill the bath, and it was Braid who soaped and washed her, her rough hands gentle against Loom's skin. Then Loom knelt over the bath as Braid poured buckets of water over her head, then massaged her scalp and kept massaging it, as though to wake some sleeping thing inside her head.

'Ma,' Loom said.

Braid fetched lengths of cloth to wrap Loom's hair and body. The fabric was orange and green and made of the heavy material she only brought out on special occasions. She wrapped Loom into it so tightly she could barely breathe.

'Pick the flame tree flowers,' Braid said.

Loom picked the crimson bells she was normally forbidden to touch and laid them on the white cloth her mother had placed on the rock outside the cabin.

They sat on the step until they heard the procession and spotted Mother Yemi, resplendent in gold, in the cart pulled by her donkey, followed by women in bright headscarves and girls with neat afros carrying treats.

'For we wel-come a daughter,' Mother Yemi sang.

'For we wel-come a daughter,' the mothers and girls sang back.

'Her new life is before her,' Mother Yemi sang.

'Her new life is before her,' they chorused.

Loom and Braid stood up.

'Give a flower to each of the mothers,' Braid said. 'If there's any left over, give them to the girls.'

Loom picked up a flower.

'Mother Yemi first,' Braid said.

There were two flowers left when the mothers all had theirs. Loom gave one to Tress and the other to Taya.

As they drank wild-grass juice and shared Loom's sweet cakes and sugar fruit, Tress whispered, 'You feel different?' She looked longingly at Loom's headscarf.

Loom touched her tummy, but shook her head.

'You'll tell us what happens . . . in the Tapestry?' Taya spoke so quietly Loom had to lean in to hear her.

'You know I would if I could,' Loom said.

Revealing what happened in the Tapestry was said to ruin a woman's destiny. Loom wasn't about to risk that, not even for her best friends.

Mother Yemi approached and placed a hand on Loom's shoulder. 'It's time.'

Loom walked towards the donkey – the same one her mother had ridden eighteen years ago – and wondered how its tired legs would carry both her and Mother Yemi.

Many arms lifted her onto the animal, seating her sideways. Braid told her where to put her feet so they didn't get caught in the wooden shaft at the donkey's side. She kissed Loom's hands, turned, and started walking back to the hut.

Loom's eyes filled with tears.

The bony creature picked its way down the steep hill, followed by the procession of women. They turned right along the path that led to Little Boat. Instead of going towards the harbour, they took the incline that led to the Tapestry, the tallest building on the island, painted yellow like the sun. The women got Loom down and helped Mother Yemi out of the cart, then Loom followed Mother Yemi to the ornate door beyond which her destiny would be decided.

'For we wel-come a daughter,' Mother Yemi sang.

The Tapestry door opened and two barefoot women stood in the doorway. 'For we wel-come a daughter,' they sang back.

'Her new life is before her,' Mother Yemi sang.

'Her new life is before her,' they echoed.

'Faith, Earnest.' Mother Yemi nodded at the two women.

They bowed, put their arms around Loom and led her into the building.

She followed them through a long water trough into a room like nothing she had seen before. The walls, ceiling and floor were covered in bright, intricate tapestries that seemed to be giving off light. Around the room, there were men working at looms. In the centre, was a chair that looked like a low-backed throne and a carving that resembled a small tree.

'Sit,' said Faith, the smaller woman, pushing Loom into the chair.

'For we wel-come a daughter . . .' the women sang.

A door at the back of the Tapestry opened and a short man with grey hair and a round stomach walked in. This had to be Pregnant Man. Loom and the other girls had heard about him. 'Her new life is before her,' he said in a flat voice.

Loom sat in the chair. The man cast his eyes over the tapestries. He raised a hand abruptly and Faith handed him a stick with a metal hook. He jabbed it into the bright weaving in front of him. Faith rushed forward, took the stick and with some twisting and sharp yanks she pulled out strands of enchanted yarn from the wall. She untangled them from the stick then handed them to Earnest.

Pregnant Man looked down and grunted. Faith rushed to him with the stick. He thrust it into part of the tapestry on the floor and left her to pull the yarn out. He continued to do this for what felt like hours, with Faith retrieving the yarn, then handing it to Earnest, who hung it on different branches of the sculpted tree.

Then, without a word, the man walked towards the wall, reached into the tapestry, opened a door, and disappeared. The men who had been silently working at the looms got up and followed him through the door.

'We'll make it special for you,' Earnest said, unwrapping Loom's hair. She put her fingers into Loom's curls and pulled so hard that Loom's eyes started to water.

Loom watched the women pick up strands of yarn, whisper to each other and return them to the tree. Whatever was in the yarn, she knew, would indicate her destiny. The

Pregnant Man had decided it. Faith turned Loom's head abruptly and the hair on her temples tightened painfully as the two women plaited scratchy lengths of yarn into it.

'She'll marry a weaver,' Earnest whispered.

'Mmm . . . They'll have two children . . . No, three,' Faith said.

'She a fisherwoman?' Earnest asked.

For a moment they let go of her head and rustled about behind her.

'No. She not like she mother.'

'She's a farmer,' Faith said.

Loom closed her eyes. A farmer – with three children, married to a weaver, who would spend his weeks in the Tapestry, which she would never be allowed to set foot in again. A weaver like her father, whom she had hardly seen before he passed. She wanted to rip the plaits from her head and run.

Tears welled in her eyes.

Faith and Earnest worked on her head through the night. At dawn, they lit yellow candles, using the melted wax to seal the bottom of Loom's plaits.

'We've wel-comed –' Faith and Earnest began, but before they could say 'a daughter', Pregnant Man appeared, carrying an engraved silver bottle.

'Be blessed,' he said, pouring oil from the bottle into his palm and sprinkling it on Loom's head.

He retreated. Faith and Earnest wrapped Loom's hair in her headscarf and tied it tightly to hold the weight of the plaits on her aching head. Then they kissed her on the cheeks and led her back to the entrance.

The light outside surged at her. She closed her eyes and took a step back, but Faith pushed her forward and a hand took hers. She knew it was her mother's. They walked together in silence along the dusty path that led to Nest Hill. Loom kept her eyes on the earth, a tightness like tangled roots in the pit of her stomach. How was she going to tell Braid that Pregnant Man had decided she was no more than a farmer?

They took the hill slowly. It seemed steeper somehow. She felt the ground undulating beneath her feet, and Braid squeezed her hand, as if to say, 'It's OK.'

When they got to their hut, Loom sat on the step while Braid unwrapped the fabric that held in her hair.

'Ah!' Braid said, holding up some plaits. 'No boats?'

Loom shook her head.

'Probably for the best. The salt air ages the skin.' Braid ran a hand across her face. 'And you're going to marry a weaver, like your mother and grandmother before you.'

Her mother walked into the hut and didn't come out for a while. Loom wound a couple of plaits around each index finger until Braid emerged, red-eyed.

'At least if destiny puts you with a so-and-so, you won't have to spend much time together,' Braid said.

She examined Loom's plaits again. Eventually she said, 'So what are you?'

'A farmer,' Loom said quietly.

'A farmer?' Braid shouted. 'You, a farmer? What farmer do you know who lives and breathes stories?'

Loom watched her mother's chest rise and fall and knew to remain silent.

'Did they mention a hidden destiny?' Braid said softly.

'What's that?' Loom said.

'Every couple of generations a woman is given a vocation, with a hidden destiny. You might be a farmer for a while, but then discover that you are meant to tell stories.'

Loom shook her head. 'They didn't mention that.'

Braid sat down on the step and covered her face with her hands. Loom put her arms around her mother. 'It's OK. I'll tell tales to the milk fruit to help them grow.'

The next day, after Braid had gone down to Little Boat, Loom made her way to school.

'Your presence is no longer required,' Mister Thomas said.

'But I still want to learn.'

'You'll learn plenty with the women in the fields.'

Loom stood there looking at him.

'Go on before Mrs Cane canes you.' He chuckled to himself and dismissed her with a wave of his arm.

Her legs were heavy as she climbed further up the hill to the fields.

Her task was to pull out the chokeweed strangling the crops. It was exhausting, but as she got into the rhythm, bending, twisting and pulling, she told stories about the farmers of old to help pass the time. The women listened and laughed and in return they helped her pull up chokeweed when Mrs Cane wasn't looking. At dusk, Loom made her way home to her cabin where her mother waited.

Braid took her in her arms and massaged her shoulders. 'You get on good?'

Loom raised her shoulders, then let them drop.

'I grilled silver,' Braid said.

Loom smiled and sat on the step to eat her favourite fish

with boiled dumplings, milk fruit and moon potatoes.

'I wish Pregnant Man had weaved a different future for you.'

Loom nodded and closed her eyes. Braid put down her plate and wiped Loom's wet cheeks with her hands.

This new rhythm in her life meant getting up early, going to tend the fields, coming home to eat with her mother, and going to bed. She missed Tress and Taya and thought about what they were learning at school while she worked the land. Her favourite time of the week was first light on Sunday before her mother got up. She would leave the cabin quietly, her hair unwrapped, and meet Tress and Taya. Then they would run down to Black Sand where Loom told them tales about sea creatures, then watched them play in the waves.

'Why don't you swim anymore?' Taya asked.

Loom pointed to her bright plaits with their yellow-wax tips.

'Well I hope The Change never comes,' Taya said.

'Hush, Taya,' Tress said. 'Do you want to remain a girl for ever?'

The rhythm of Loom's life stayed the same until a month after she turned fifteen. She got back from the fields and found Braid leaning against the cabin, almost doubled over, coughing. She rushed to her mother and massaged her back, then fetched the jug and poured her a cup of water.

Braid coughed some more and then took a sip.

'Has it passed?' Loom said.

Braid nodded and Loom tucked her into the bed they shared.

The next day, when she came home her mother was

already in bed.

The blood came a few weeks later. Braid tried not to let Loom see the red on the cloth she put to her mouth when she coughed.

Loom began getting up earlier to help her mother get ready for work and insisted on walking her down to the harbour.

A few weeks later she came home from the fields and Braid wasn't there. Loom went to the yard out back and called for her, but there was no answer. She raced to Little Boat.

A crowd of women huddled near the moored boats. Loom pushed her way through and saw Braid propped up on a colourful tapestry.

'It is as it was woven,' Mother Yemi said. 'No more fishing for her. She can't take the sea air. Help her up to her hut. Let her rest there.'

The women shooed Loom out of the way.

She rushed up the hill ahead of them to light the lantern and pull down the sheets for her mother.

'No need to fuss, I fine,' Braid said, when she was back in their cabin.

For a few weeks, the women passed by in the evening with food, then one by one they stopped coming. When Loom ran into them in the market they wouldn't meet her eyes.

Loom started working seven days in the fields instead of five, but it still wasn't enough to provide for the two of them. Every now and then Tress would come by with a little parcel of food, but Loom knew her family couldn't spare it, so she would send it away. She kept asking herself why she had to be a farmer when her talent was for cultivating words. And why was her mother a fisherwoman when she knew numbers better than anyone?

If she were a storyteller, she could earn enough for them both. Just a couple of engagements a month would pay far more than she could ever earn toiling every day in the fields.

One evening, on her way back home, she bumped into Taya who was sweeping the ground outside her cabin. Taya put her arms around her and then gently felt her ribs. She shook her head. 'The Tapestry changed you.' She placed a hand on Loom's headscarf and felt the plaits beneath it. 'Shame you can't just take them out.'

If women undid the life stories woven into their hair, they died. Everyone knew about Spool, the woman from the other side of the island who undid her plaits and dropped down dead that very night.

But what would happen if Loom undid just *one*?

The next day after working the fields, she went to find Mother Yemi, who lived in the grand brick house at the top of Sunset Hill. Loom brought a flower from the flame tree by her cabin to bless the old woman. Mother Yemi sat alone on the porch, drinking from a tall glass of wild-grass juice and eating rarenuts.

Loom had never been this close to a brick house before, let alone a double-fronted one with two floors. There was a stone path in front that cut through an immaculate lawn, surrounded by sky bushes laden with velvet petals. It was all contained by a white picket fence with a large gate.

Loom called from the street.

When Mother Yemi beckoned, she opened the gate, closing it carefully behind her, then made her way up to the porch, where she bowed and handed Mother Yemi the flower.

'Can you help me?'

'That depends.' Mother Yemi sniffed the red petals. 'What kind of help are you seeking?'

'I need to know which bit of the weaving in my hair means I'm a farmer,' Loom said.

'Why do you come to me with such questions?'

Loom massaged Mother Yemi's shoulders as she'd seen her mother do.

'Not just anyone has that kind of learning,' Loom said. 'Few can read the weaving just so.' She craned her neck to see whether her words were having an effect on Mother Yemi. 'Am I correct in thinking you're the only woman on the island who knows how to read *all* the weaving?'

Mother Yemi straightened in her chair.

'I heard that you read weaving better than most men.' Loom saw the beginnings of a smile on Mother Yemi's round face. 'They say that you are an expert reader –'

'Flattery holds no sway with me,' Mother Yemi said.

Loom looked down at the floor, her hands resting on Mother Yemi's shoulders.

'Don't stop,' the old woman said.

She wasn't sure whether Mother Yemi meant don't stop the massage or the flattery, so she continued with both. 'I bet I'm correct in thinking you are the most expert reader on this island.'

'Fetch the looking glass from beside my bed,' Mother Yemi said.

Loom dusted off her feet and hesitated at the door.

'There's no snake in there to bite you,' Mother Yemi said. 'Go.'

Loom ran in, the tiles cold beneath her feet. Ahead of

her was a wide staircase with a gleaming wooden banister. Loom wasn't sure where Mother Yemi's bedroom was, so she opened one of the two doors on her left. It was a bright room four times the size of her cabin, with cream sofas and armchairs, and portraits of families dressed in finery on the walls. The second room was a study with a large desk, and hundreds of books. On the other side of the hallway, there was a dining room with a long polished table. The fourth room turned out to be a kitchen with marble countertops. A thin woman in an apron was washing dishes under running water.

'Mother Yemi's room?' Loom said quickly.

The woman looked her up and down. 'Upstairs. First door on the right.'

She ran up the stairs and found the vast bedroom with a long balcony overlooking the sea. Behind the bed was a tapestry of the island with every cabin and house. Loom grabbed the mirror.

'Did you get lost?' Mother Yemi said, frowning. 'Sit and hold up the glass.'

She pulled Loom down in front of her and unwrapped her headscarf. 'You see these strands here?' She held up a plait that looked like a yellow flower emerging from a plant rooted in the mud. 'They mean you are a farmer. Look how the green weaves into the yellow, surrounded by brown in that pattern there.' Mother Yemi ran her hand down the length of the plait. 'You're not like your mother. You'll farm until the end of your days.'

Loom nodded slowly.

'It's a shame though,' Mother Yemi said. 'I heard about the stories you tell . . . But the weaving's the weaving and it says you're a farmer.'

'Perhaps I have a hidden destiny?' Loom said, barely audibly.

Mother Yemi searched through Loom's plaits, lifting and dropping a few at a time. After a while she said, 'No.'

'How come Pregnant Man gets to decide?' Loom asked.

'His name is Mister Yarn.' Mother Yemi looked at her for a moment with narrowed eyes. 'He has the sacred authority. It was passed down to him.'

'But why does he make it so Nest Hill women are only farmers or fisherwomen? Why can't we be storytellers or –'

'Because that's not what he sees in the tapestry.' Mother Yemi frowned. 'You're a farmer. The weaving says so.'

'What if I took that plait out? What if I changed it?' Loom said, glancing up at Mother Yemi.

'Then you would drop down dead. You understand? You would surely die. You've got no business messing with the weaving. No business at all.' Mother Yemi's voice had a sharpness to it that Loom had never heard before.

'But why do girls in some families get to become doctors and storytellers, while the rest of us –'

Mother Yemi struggled to her feet and waved towards Nest Hill. 'Go home. Your mother needs you.'

Loom bowed, turned on her heels and ran home.

Loom returned from the fields one evening with a bag of overripe milk fruit that had been given to her by Mrs Cane, who'd prodded her ribs and said she was scrawny. She cooked just enough for her mother. She had to make them last. She missed the days when she would come home to freshly grilled fish. Braid had worked harder than most other islanders and all she got in return was a little earth seed.

What if she just undid the *end* of the braid that made her a farmer? That wouldn't kill her, would it?

On a day when the dirt track scorched her feet, she arrived at the fields to find Mrs Cane standing under a tree fanning herself. As Mrs Cane mopped her brow, she started yelling, though not at anyone in particular. Then she saw Loom.

'I give her plenty milk fruit, but she's still skin and bone. How am I supposed to grow fine earth seed with this skeleton?'

She made Loom work harder than the others and when the women took their break under the shade of a tree, Mrs Cane found her more chokeweed to pull.

That night, while her mother slept, Loom went outside, lit the lantern and sat on the step. She took up her mirror and found the green plait, woven into yellow, surrounded by brown. Holding it in one hand, she fetched a knife and cut off the bottom of the plait, where it was fused together with candle wax. She checked herself. She did not feel any different. With tentative fingers she began to undo it. Once she'd loosened an inch or so, she checked her pulse – racing but fine; breathing, fast, but fine. She extinguished the lantern and went back to bed, but wouldn't let herself sleep in case she didn't wake again.

She rose late in the morning. She felt the same as she had the previous day. That night she went outside and sat on the step. She said a prayer, then began to undo more of the plait, her scalp aching as she pulled at the yarn. She kept undoing it until only soft black curls remained. She rubbed the freed hair between her fingers as she tried to slow her breathing.

When she went to bed, island stories about Spool dying

after taking out her plaits circled in her mind. She tossed and turned, sweat dampening her nightgown until finally she succumbed to sleep. Late morning, she opened her eyes and started to giggle. If the enchanted yarn had made her a farmer, she was a farmer no more.

'Mother Yemi,' she called, as she entered the old woman's front garden, her hastily wrapped hair leaning to one side. 'Mother Yemi, am I a ghost?'

'I doubt it,' Mother Yemi said from her seat on the porch. 'I never did meet one so noisy.'

Loom went up to the old woman and whispered in her ear. 'I undid the weaving that says I am a farmer.'

'You did what! You're too young to die. Too young . . .'

'I'm not dead, Mother Yemi. I'm as alive as you.' She reached for Mother Yemi's hand and held it in her own.

'You're breathing now, but it's sure to kill you in the night.' Mother Yemi rocked in her chair and moaned.

'But I undid the weaving yesterday.'

Mother Yemi turned and frowned at Loom. 'Yesterday?'

Loom nodded.

Mother Yemi made her sit and examined her hair. Then she pinched Loom's nose closed, forcing her to breathe through her mouth.

'I want to be a storyteller,' Loom said.

'I saw Spool's body – stiff and cold,' Mother Yemi muttered to herself, as though she hadn't heard. 'They said she died because she tried to change her destiny. I thought it was the enchanted yarn.' She shook her head.

Finally, she stood up. 'Come back tomorrow afternoon,' she said.

*

131

When Loom reached the porch the next day, Mother Yemi handed her a plate of meaty crescent fish and a cup of wild-grass juice. 'Do you know who my husband is?' she said, without meeting Loom's eyes.

Loom shook her head.

'Mister Yarn.'

Loom's eyes widened.

'Eat,' Mother Yemi said.

Loom broke open a crescent fish, sucked it and pulled out the flesh with her teeth. It was delicious. Why had she never tried it before?

'I know how to get the enchanted yarn,' Mother Yemi said.

Loom stared at her.

'And I know how to weave hair.'

'You worked in the Tapestry?'

'Exactly so,' Mother Yemi said. 'How do you think I met my husband?'

Mother Yemi shuffled into her house and emerged with a box. She lifted the lid and revealed brightly coloured yarn on a bed of white satin. 'If you don't want to be a farmer, I can make it so. Sit!'

Mother Yemi began humming. Loom recognised the tune of 'We wel-come a daughter', only it sounded mournful. Gently, Mother Yemi began to plait the yarn into Loom's hair.

When she was finished, Mother Yemi rubbed her hands on Loom's skirts and said, 'I have given you a hidden destiny. You must never try to change your hair again.' She looked Loom straight in the eyes. 'Your life depends on it.'

'What have you made me?' Loom said.

'See this plait that is blue, woven into green and aqua?'

Mother Yemi gave the plait to Loom so that she could examine it. 'It means your hidden destiny is to weave hair.'

Loom stared at Mother Yemi, then her eyes dropped down to the earth, cracked and dry beneath her bare feet.

Deadlifting

Nicholas Kemp

It's the morning of the Classic and Ash's dad is making breakfast. He cracks six eggs into a jug and pours in a whole bottle of full-fat milk. Then he opens a tin of brewer's yeast and dumps two mountainous tablespoons of sandy-brown powder over the milky eggs.

'When Darren and I were training,' he says, 'we used to have this six, seven times a day. It's quick, it's cheap, and it bulks you up like nobody's business.'

He whisks the mixture together and pours it into two dimpled pint mugs. He sets one of the mugs in front of Ash and the other in front of himself.

'Bottoms up,' he says, raising his mug to his lips.

Ash looks doubtfully at the drink in front of him. It's grey, thick, and fizzing with fat, foamy bubbles. Undissolved clumps of yeast bob about on the surface. It smells a bit like custard, a bit like bread, a bit like vomit.

'Come on, son,' says his dad. 'Get it down you.'

Half of his dad's drink has already disappeared. There's a grey, creamy residue around his mouth and a line of gloopy fluid running down the outside of his mug.

Ash grabs the handle of his pint. The taste is even worse

than he thought it would be. It's like jumping into freezing water: that sudden realisation when you plunge through the surface that it's more painfully cold than you could possibly imagine. Ash fights hard not to throw up as he forces gulp after gulp of slimy, chunky liquid down his throat. Trickles spill from his mouth and dribble down his chin.

Darren's not picking them up till eight o'clock, so they've got plenty of time to work out. Ash hasn't had a chance to work out with his dad for ages. He's been putting in extra sessions on his own for the last few weeks, and he wants to show off how many sets he can do.

The garage lights plink on. Ash's dad heaves plates onto his barbell.

'We'll start small today,' he says. 'Then see how we get on.'

Ash's mum won't let him use his dad's weights until he turns fourteen. She's promised to smack him into the middle of next week if he so much as touches them before his fourteenth birthday. She says that if Ash lifts weights before his balls drop, he won't grow. It happened to a boy she knew at school.

Sweat boils off his dad's forehead. Veins stand out on his arms like brass rubbings. He swears as he lifts, stretching out the syllables of the swear words as if they're made of elastic.

'Shiiiiiiiiiiiiiiiiiiiiiiiiiiiiiiiiiiiiiiiiiiiiiiiiiiiiiiiiiiiiiit.'

'Baaaaaaaaaaaaaaaaaaaaastaaaaaaaaaaaaaaaaaaaaaaaard.'

'Waaaaaaaaaaaaaaaaaaaaaaaaaaaaaaankeeeeeeeeeeeeeer.'

There's a spiderweb crack in the concrete where one of the heaviest plates slipped off the barbell and crashed to the floor. His mum said that if Ash had been under it, it would have caved his skull in.

By the time his dad finishes his deadlifts, his muscles are twitching like frogs' legs. He's in pain, but that's the point. He's told Ash that muscles only get bigger if you hurt them. You need to damage the fibres so they can grow back stronger. Agony means you're going in the right direction.

It's Ash's turn to work out now. He unrolls his mat and begins his callisthenics.

'Watch your form,' says his dad. 'If it's not perfect, you're only cheating yourself.'

Under his dad's gaze, Ash cycles through sit-ups, press-ups, calf raises, squats and tricep dips. His muscles plump up with blood. His pecs feel tight and achy in a way he's started to love.

'Your squat's all wrong,' says his dad. 'Your spine is curving forward.'

'I thought I was keeping it straight?'

His dad holds out his hand and bends his fingers to form an open bracket.

'This is what your back looks like. If you tried lifting any weight with a backbone like that, you'd end up in the hospital.'

Ash wishes his dad could see the squats he did yesterday. Those squats were perfect, and he had done so many of them. If his dad had seen them, he would have been proud.

'Do it again. I'm not having you squatting like that when you're older.'

Ash does as he's told. He plants his feet on the mat, a fraction wider than his hips, and sticks out his bottom. He tightens his abs. He tries to hold his back as straight as possible. With outstretched arms, he bends at the knees.

'Your head's too far forward.'

'Sorry, Dad.'

'And your back keeps bending when you dip.'

'Sorry, Dad.'

'Stop saying sorry. Just get it right.'

Darren's waiting for them outside. He's sitting in the driver's seat of his Transit van, taking up so much space that Ash doesn't know how they're all going to fit in.

'We used to call Daz the South London Lou Ferrigno,' Ash's dad told him. 'He was that muscular. But when he stopped lifting, it all turned to fat.'

Darren rolls down the window and asks Ash to hit him a bicep. Ash obliges, and the smile on Darren's face is enormous, like a mouth carved in a pumpkin.

'Your boy's looking massive,' says Darren. 'He's not started juicing, has he?'

Inside the cab, Ash can smell the vinegary smell of Darren's BO and the eggy smell of his farts. Ash has got the middle seat, and he's crushed between the heavy flesh of the two big men. On his lap, he cradles his copy of *The New Encyclopedia of Modern Bodybuilding*.

'What you brought that old thing for?' says Darren.

'I'm going to get him to sign it,' says Ash.

'Who?'

'Arnold,' says Ash.

Who else?

Ash's dad is asleep by the time they reach the motorway. The seat belt clamps his pecs like the hoop around a wooden barrel. Ash's dad is proud of his pecs. He calls them his 'Gorillas'. He used to make Ash laugh by jiggling his Gorillas in time to the *Simpsons* theme tune.

Darren watches the road, his huge belly sitting on top of him.

'So, Ash,' he says, 'you excited to meet Arnie?'

'Yeah.'

'How many Mr Olympias did he win again?'

'Seven.'

'Wasn't it six?'

'No,' says Ash. 'It was seven. He won six in a row before retiring in 1975. Then he came back to win his seventh while he was training for *Conan the Barbarian*.'

'*Conan the Barbarian*,' says Darren, wistfully. 'Now that's a movie.'

'Is it good?'

Darren stares at Ash.

'You mean, you've not seen it?' he says.

Ash's parents won't let him. He's seen all of Arnold's PGs, Us and 12s, but he's not allowed to watch any of the 15s and 18s. Ash thinks this is unfair, even more unfair than his mum's stupid weightlifting rule. For about a year, he's been scanning the TV listings in the paper, hunting for any late-night showings of Arnold's films. He waits till his parents are asleep, then he creeps down to the living room and turns on the telly. He's seen *The Terminator*, *Eraser*, *Predator*, and *Commando*. He's been caught only once. His mum walked in on him halfway through *Total Recall* and shouted so loudly that she woke the neighbour's dog.

Darren changes gear. In his massive hand, the gear stick looks as small as a lollipop.

He says, 'Your dad and I saw *Conan* when it came out in the cinema. It was the first time we saw Arnold moving, not just pictures of him in magazines. We were blown away. Here was this bloke, rippling all over with big, beautiful muscles, holding this giant broadsword and killing every old fucker in his way.'

Ash's dad starts snoring, his head lolling against the window.

'You know,' says Darren, 'he's been really looking forward to going to the Classic with you.'

'Dad?' says Ash.

Darren nods.

'He's not shut up about it for weeks.'

'You can cheat a bench press, you can cheat on the barbells, but you can't cheat a deadlift.'

'There's no hiding with the deadlift. You can either lift it or you can't.'

'If you want to see how strong a bloke is, get him to deadlift for you.'

'It's what separates the men from the boys.'

'When you've finished a set of heavy deadlifts, the pump you get is better than jizzing.'

'The boy's twelve years old, Daz.'

'Sorry, Ken.'

The three of them are in Hall 5 of the Birmingham NEC, where they're watching the deadlift finals at the Arnold Classic. Their seats are towards the back of the hall, past rows and rows of people who look more or less like Darren and Ash's dad.

The next powerlifter takes the stage, and the MC calls out his name through a microphone. It's a long, foreign name. Its syllables are segmented like a centipede. All Ash can make out is the first name: Nicu.

His dad and Darren are on their feet along with the rest of the spectators.

'This bloke's got the world record,' says his dad. 'He's won Europe's Strongest Man three years in a row and World's Strongest Man twice.'

'You should see his girlfriend,' says Darren. 'She's like a Page 3 girl.'

Nicu is quite comfortably the largest man Ash has ever seen in his life. He's even bigger than Darren. He's got thighs for arms, a bowling-ball belly, beef-shank pecs, and a bald head that squeezes out of his shoulders like a hernia.

'Come on, son,' shouts Darren. 'Give 'em hell!'

Nicu sidles up to the barbell. The plates on his bar dwarf the ones Ash's dad lifted that morning. These plates are the size of tractor tyres.

The referee gives the signal and Nicu grabs the bar. He moves into position. With his fat gut lowered between his legs, and his face scrunched up in concentration, he looks like he's laying an egg.

'Watch how he keeps his back straight,' says Ash's dad.

Nicu's enormous body goes rigid, every muscle quivering with intent. He drives with his legs and pushes himself upwards. His back couldn't be straighter. His spine looks like it's made of iron.

'Have it!' cheers Ash's dad, as the barbell pulls away from the ground.

Nicu only manages to lift up the bar for a few seconds, but to Ash it seems much longer, like a moment suspended out of time. When Nicu finally lets go, he staggers back from the mat. He looks drained, shocked, and Ash thinks he's going

141

to pass out. But then he turns to face the spectators and roars.

Ash's dad squeezes Ash's shoulder.

'Ashley,' he says, 'you've just seen the strongest man in the world.'

Three years later, Ash is in the attic when he finds photos from his dad's weightlifting days. His mum's asked him to bring down a suitcase, and as he's heaving it from behind the water tank, he spots the yellow corner of a Tripleprint envelope in a box of Christmas decorations. His dad is a young man in the photos. He's shirtless, oiled up, and he's showing off his lifts at the gym. His weights are heavy, and his form is perfect. His poses could be illustrations from Ash's *Encyclopedia*.

Ash has never seen his dad's physique look so glorious. His biceps have peaks. His back is a mountain range. His Gorillas are wonderfully striated. He's got beautiful serratus muscles flanking his abs. Ash knows how hard these are to develop. Every day for the last few months, he's been doing set after set of closed-grip chin-ups to try and beef up his own.

Ash has been training properly ever since he turned fourteen. Three times a week he works out in the garage with his dad's old bench and barbell, and on Saturdays and Sundays, he lifts at the gym while Darren gives pointers on his form. He's started eating properly too. He's cut out all complex carbohydrates, and he won't have anything processed. He gets annoyed when his mum cooks him sausages for dinner.

Ash's mum is in the garden with his auntie, chatting about their summer holidays. Tommy, Ash's cousin, is playing a noisy game of superheroes on the lawn. He's wearing his Captain America mask, and he's beating up scores of invisible Hydra agents.

When Ash's mum sees the photos, she puts her hand to her mouth and makes a noise that's somewhere between a squeal and a gasp.

'Where did you find this, Ash?'

'In the attic.'

'I haven't seen these for years.'

She's staring at a picture of Ash's dad executing a flawless clean and press. His body looks just like the Gold's Gym silhouette.

'How old was he then?' asks Ash.

'He must have been twenty-one. Yeah, that's right. I got him those trainers for his twenty-first.'

His mum starts laughing. It's wild, joyous laughter, and she has to wipe tears from her eyes when she's finished.

'He and Daz had this plan to send their pics into one of the fitness magazines. Your dad thought they'd make a bit of money. You should have heard him when he found out they only wanted Darren's shots.'

Tommy abandons his superhero game and bounds over to the patio to see what all the fuss is about.

'Who's that?' he says bossily.

'It's Ash's dad, Tom.'

Tommy takes off his Captain America mask so he can get a better look.

'He looks indestructible,' he says.

A shiver runs up Ash's spine.

'He was,' says Ash's mum. 'He really, really was.'

The queue for the Meet and Greet is a painfully slow-moving

glacier of Arnold fans. It snakes practically all the way around the inside of the exhibition centre. Ash casts his connoisseur's eye over the memorabilia in the fans' eager arms. There are posters of *Pumping Iron*, *Stay Hungry* and *Terminator 2*, as well as DVDs of *Last Action Hero*, *Twins* and *Kindergarten Cop*. There are Turbo Man action figures, Predator masks and copies of Arnold's fitness books. Just behind them, a narrow-shouldered man clutches a photograph of a Muscle Beach-era Arnold in tiny bikini briefs.

Ash has never been more excited to meet anyone in his life. He's been rehearsing the conversation with Arnold ever since his dad gave him the tickets. He's even written it down.

'Mr Schwarzenegger, can you sign my *Encyclopedia*?'

'Of course, young man, I'd love to.'

'I read it all the time.'

'Really? That's a tremendous honour coming from such a well-built guy like you.'

'Have you ever been to Bermondsey?'

'No, but I'm shooting a movie in London next year, and I have plans to open a gym in Bermondsey. I'll train there every day.'

'When you come to London, can I spot you?'

'Absolutely. You read my mind.'

Ash's dad takes the tickets out of his pocket and hands them to a lady at the entrance of the Meet and Greet hall. A light bulb flashes red when the lady puts the tickets through the scanner. It's an ominous red: the same dim, deep colour of the Terminator's eyes.

'I'm sorry, sir,' says the lady, 'but these aren't the right tickets.'

'What do you mean?' says Ash's dad. 'How are they not right?'

'You can't get into the Meet and Greet with these tickets. These are for the events and the exhibitions. They're basic entry.'

'The bloke who sold them to me told me they were good for the Meet and Greet.'

The lady shakes her head. She holds up the tickets to his dad's face and points to the writing.

'It says "Basic Entry" right here at the bottom. The tickets for the Meet and Greet say "Meet and Greet" at the bottom.'

'Well, then,' says his dad, 'how much for the Meet and Greet tickets?'

'I'm sorry, sir. Those tickets all sold out in twenty-four hours.'

'This is fucking unbelievable.'

Ash's dad swears a lot, but Ash knows that he only uses the F-word when he's seriously angry. Darren must have noticed it too because now he steps in front of Ash's dad.

'Look, love,' he says. 'Is there no way you can just let us through? The little lad just wants to meet his hero.'

'I'm sorry, sir,' says the lady, 'but I can't let you go through without the right tickets.'

'This is a fucking joke,' says Ash's dad. 'We're right at the front of the fucking queue. We've got the tickets and we're fucking going in.'

He's shouting now. Ash hates it when his dad shouts. It's a burst blood vessel voice that used to scare him as a child. Ash thinks that it's scaring the lady as well because she's beckoning over a security guard. The guard is huge. He could be a powerlifter himself. His gym-heavy shoulders are the same height as his dad's head.

'Sir,' says the guard. 'I'm going to have to ask you to calm down.'

'My son needs to meet Arnold. I promised him he'd meet Arnold.'

His dad's not shouting anymore. His voice sounds desperate.

'Not today, pal,' says the guard. 'If you won't leave, I'll have to escort you out.'

'Please. You don't know what it means to him.'

Six months later, Ash goes with his mum to visit his dad in the hospital. His dad's been in the hospital a lot recently, but this is the first time he's had to be taken there in an ambulance.

'It's just a little infection,' says his mum. 'They're just being extra safe because his immune system's a bit wobbly at the moment.'

In the hospital, Ash and his mum slip on latex gloves and tie plastic aprons around their waists. It's just like *ER*. His mum and dad love *ER*. They've got all the DVDs stacked up in a tower by the telly. Ash's mum helps Ash with his face mask, hooking the elastic cords behind his ears and squeezing the wire bridge onto his nose.

A nurse leads them down a corridor and shows them to the room where Ash's dad is being looked after.

For a moment, Ash thinks there's been some sort of mistake. The man lying in the hospital bed doesn't look like his dad. His dad is big and strong, and this man is a weakling. His torso is nothing but a rib cage in skin and hospital pyjamas.

'Ashley,' hisses his mum, 'say something for God's sake.'

'He's just frightened. It must be a shock to see me like this.'

There's no mistaking his dad's voice, but it's laboured as if every word is a struggle.

Ash's mum sits down on a chair a few feet away from the bed. She starts talking to this frail version of his dad about the neighbours, about how Ash's doing at school, about what happened at work that week. The sentences pour out of her as if she's trying to fill up a bath. Now and then her glasses fog with steam and she has to take them off and rub them on her apron.

'That's great, love,' says his dad. 'It sounds like one hell of a week.'

His mum starts crying. They're loud, noisy tears, like when she watches the John Lewis adverts at Christmas.

'I didn't think it would get like this, Ken,' she says. 'I didn't know.'

'It's all right,' says his dad. 'It's all going to be OK, love.'

Ash's mum goes outside, and now Ash is alone in the room with his dad. There are the sounds of the machines beeping and whirring by his bed.

'How's your training going?' says his dad. 'How's your form?'

His dad's lips are dry and chapped. The skin around his mouth looks raw.

'Ash. You just can't be scared like this anymore.'

'I'm sorry,' says Ash. 'But I'm terrified.'

'You can't be.'

'Sorry.'

'Stop saying sorry.'

His dad pauses.

'Remember when we went to the Classic? Remember when we saw that lifter smash the world record?'

Ash nods. He remembers it perfectly. He remembers his dad telling him that he'd just seen the strongest man in the

147

world, and he remembers him squeezing his shoulder. He thought that his dad was showing him something then, as if his hand squeezing his shoulder was his dad's way of guiding him into the world of men.

'Do you remember what he's called?'

Ash looks straight into his dad's eyes and says, 'Nicu Asparukhov.'

Ash had Googled Nicu's name as soon as he got home from the Classic, saying it over and over to himself to commit it to memory. Over the next few weeks, he searched online for clips of Nicu's squats and deadlifts. He watched the videos on repeat, copying Nicu's form precisely, so that his dad might notice the improvement when they next worked out together.

'You need to be like Nicu,' says his dad. 'You've got to keep your back straight and your eyes in front of you. You've got to drive from your legs, Ash. You got to drive from your legs and lift.'

Before Ash realises what he's doing, he's ducked beneath the security guard's arm and he's burst through the double doors of the Meet and Greet hall. He's only faintly aware that his dad is yelling after him. He's running as fast as he can.

Ash doesn't recognise Arnold immediately because he's so much older than the posters on his bedroom wall. His face is lined. His skin is waxy. His hair is a strange soy-sauce colour, and it's noticeably thinning at the front. But as soon as he opens his mouth, Ash has no doubts who it is. No one else in the whole world has a voice like that.

Arnold Schwarzenegger wears a shiny bomber jacket, dark jeans and a black T-shirt. A fat gold watch peeks out from his sleeve. He's standing alone on a raised platform, and behind him there's a white background with the name of the Classic written on it in chrome-coloured letters.

An assistant brings up a pair of fans to meet him.

Arnold shakes their hands and says, 'Nice to meet you,' and 'Good to see you,' and 'Thank you for being here.'

His voice sounds so real, Ash thinks it could be an MP3 of him talking. The fans look up at him like two disciples meeting their god.

'We've always wanted to meet you,' they say. 'We've seen all your films.'

The assistant tells the fans to stand on either side of Arnold while he takes their picture. Then another assistant leads them off the platform.

'Thank you,' says Arnold. 'Enjoy the rest of the Classic.'

The whole meeting is over in under a minute.

Ash shouts Arnold's name much louder than he means to, and everyone turns in the direction of the noise. Arnold was smiling when he was greeting his fans but now his face has hardened. It's the same grim expression he wore when he bazookaed that jeep in *Commando*.

Arnold says, 'What do you want?' and Ash can feel the blood pumping in his ears. He holds up his *Encyclopedia* and asks Arnold if he can sign it. But he's so nervous that the question comes out of his mouth as one word: 'Arnoldcanyousignmyencyclopedia?'

'No,' says Arnold, firmly. 'You need to have a ticket if you want me to sign anything.'

'My dad got me a ticket,' says Ash. 'But it's the wrong one.'

Arnold shrugs.

'Then that is his problem. Not mine.'

Ash feels an enormous hand wrapping around his upper

149

arm. He looks up and sees the powerlifter security guard.

'You have to sign my book, Arnold,' says Ash. 'And you have to do it now.'

Arnold looks surprised.

'Are you giving me an order?'

'Yes, I am.'

Arnold smiles.

'What's your name?'

'Ash.'

Arnold repeats his name, but in his Arnold accent it sounds like 'Atch'.

'Give me your book, Atch,' he says.

Ash wriggles out of the security guard's grip. He strides over to the platform and hands Arnold his copy of the *Encyclopedia*. He's embarrassed that he's not looked after it better. Its corners are dog-eared and peeling, and the pages fan upwards like leaves looking for the sun. Arnold, however, doesn't seem to mind. Maybe he's flattered that the book bears the scars of so much reading. He pulls out a Sharpie from the pocket of his bomber jacket and pops off the lid. The pen makes a dry, squeaky sound as he signs his autograph.

'There,' he says, handing back the book. 'Your *Encyclopedia*, Atch.'

Arnold's accent transforms the word 'encyclopedia' into something extraordinary, like the Latin name for a set of powerful muscles.

Ash is as close to Arnold right now as he was to the posters in his bedroom when he was practising his conversation.

'Have you ever been to Bermondsey?' he asks.

'No,' says Arnold.

'Are you going to open a gym there?'

'I don't think so.'

'If you do come, my dad and I can spot you.'

Arnold gestures to someone behind Ash, and moments later the security guard is gripping Ash's arm once again. Ash is being pulled slowly away from Arnold. The heels of his trainers drag along the floor.

'My dad's really good at deadlifting,' says Ash. 'He can help you out with your form.'

'That's terrific, Atch,' says Arnold. 'Maybe I'll ask him someday.'

Ash's dad gave him *The New Encyclopedia of Modern Bodybuilding* the Christmas before last. It's the best present he's ever been given, and that's especially surprising because his dad has always been terrible at giving presents.

His mum made a bit of a stink when she saw what was beneath the wrapping paper.

'We spoke about this, Ken,' she said. 'Not till he turns fourteen.'

'It's the best book you can buy,' said his dad. 'Daz and I used it all the time when we were training.'

'But he's too young.'

'It's not for now. It's for later. He'll need something to tell him what to do if I'm not around.'

His mum rolled her eyes.

'What are you on about?' she said. 'What's all this "if I'm not around" business?'

'All I'm saying is, it's good for the boy to know what he can achieve if he sets his mind to it.'

'Give it a rest, Mr Motivator,' said Ash's mum. 'And put the bloody kettle on.'

Ash held the *Encyclopedia* in his hands, acquainting himself with its heft. It was a heavy book, but a book by Arnold should be heavy. It should make your wrists ache if you hold it for too long.

In the van, Darren and his dad are pissing themselves as Ash tells them the story. This is now the fourth time he's told it, and they've only just joined the motorway out of Birmingham.

Ash is adding bits to it, making it wilder and more outlandish. Now he's kicking the security guard down a flight of stairs. Now Arnold's asking Ash to hit biceps and show him his quads. Now, Ash is being offered roles in *Terminator 5* and the *Conan* reboot. His dad and Darren are loving it and they're egging him on.

'In all my dreams,' says Darren, 'I did not think that your son would have the brass bollocks to pull off a stunt like that.'

'I shall be telling that story,' says his dad proudly, 'for the rest of my days.'

Ash's dad opens the *Encyclopedia* and stares at the thick, black squiggles of Arnold's signature. He traces it with the tip of his finger, then kisses Ash on the cheek. It's a small, quiet kiss, but Ash feels the pressure of it for a long time afterwards, like the pain he feels in his legs when he's done too many squats.

'Bloody well done, son,' says his dad.

There's a black-and-white picture of Arnold on the front cover of the *Encyclopedia*. It's Ash's favourite picture of Arnold – it could very well be his favourite picture of anything. Ash has copied the pose in that picture a hundred times in the bathroom mirror. It's Arnold in his glorious prime, proudly contemplating his shockingly well-developed bicep. What Ash likes most about the picture is the fact that it's in black and white. It makes the skin on Arnold's muscles look shiny and liquid, like mercury sliding over rock.

Overworld

Kate Horsley

Adrian looked back at his old road: brown bins lined up unevenly on the pavement, a couple of satellite dishes, their bright, white faces tilted upwards. Those same hollow streams of traffic from Barry Road. The lights were on upstairs. He didn't like to think about what had gone on inside. He'd said it to himself so many times – he'd felt like a different person, not remotely like his normal self. But the justifications frustrated him now just as much as they always had done. The words were facile, palpably inadequate, a stupid foil for what he suspected was a far less palatable truth. When he was in his new flat he could forget about some of it – he'd managed to fit himself into a type of soothing, protective rhythm. He was sleeping again. He'd started running around Belair Park. Tammy didn't drink during the week. She'd given up red meat, too. He'd quickly adapted to her preferences but none of it felt sacrificial. If anything, every time he'd noticed another of her careful, reflective habits, he'd felt a small, distinct thrill.

Adrian opened the gate and moved towards the door. A note had been Sellotaped above the bell. He recognised Oliver's small, effortful handwriting. *No junk mail*. He thought about the subject header of the first email Harriet had sent him after he'd moved out. *Does Oliver need psychotherapy?* He could remember the shape of the message on the screen, the 'Dear Adrian', the exacting punctuation, each assiduous comma and full stop a discreet, absurd blow. He remembered the phrasing, too: Oliver's teacher had said that he was no longer 'meeting expectations'. He'd become 'withdrawn', his handwriting was getting smaller to the 'point of illegibility'. Adrian was still staring at his son's note.

'Adrian Ward! Thought it was you! Recognised the car.' Michael was a wiry fifty-year-old with a narrow, bright set of eyes. 'How you keeping, then? Back on the old stomping ground!'

'Picking up Oliver,' Adrian called back.

'Forecast's saying storms, you know,' Michael said. He lifted his jaw upwards. 'Taking him out for the day, are you?'

'That's the plan,' Adrian said.

'Wind and rain all day is what they're saying.' He nodded at the curtained windows. 'Make sure she puts him in proper clothes. Kids'll complain about anything if you give them half a chance.'

Adrian smiled weakly. He didn't like the idea of Michael watching them, the seedily nostalgic partaking of his family's reunions. He took a breath, steadying himself. Harriet had stopped all the shouting a few months ago but her anger had morphed into something more threatening, a stiff and unyielding coldness which carried with it an air of unpredictability. Adrian pressed on the bell. Tammy had been asleep when he'd left, one side of her face resting on her hand. He'd thought she might wake up with pins and needles so he'd slowly prised the hand out from under her. She was a heavy sleeper and nothing in her expression registered the intrusion.

Footsteps moved with careful purpose along the hallway, the chain along its track.

'Hi,' Harriet said. She smiled. She was wearing the quilted jacket he'd bought her for her fortieth.

'Hiya,' Adrian said. He checked across the street. Michael had gone back inside.

'Ol,' Harriet shouted. 'Dad's here!'

'I'm just charging my phone,' the boy shouted down. 'Two minutes.'

Harriet shut the door and stepped down into the small front garden. Grey flinty shavings covered most of the soil; in summer, geraniums flowered from smooth clay pots. 'Quick chat OK?' Harriet said.

'Sure.'

She'd had her hair cut shorter. Her face looked thinner, her eyes a little larger or darker perhaps. Or perhaps it was the expression behind her eyes which was different, a placid, equable self-possession.

'OK,' Harriet began. She'd arranged her hands tidily. 'I want to keep things civil, Adrian. And that's not just lip service. I really mean it this time.' She smiled again. 'I had my final session with my therapist last week.' She shivered. 'Anyway, *I'm* going to explain things to Oliver. I think it's for the best.'

'I was going to talk to him today.'

'Today?'

'Today.'

'You've been saying that for a little while now, though, Ade,' Harriet said.

'I promise,' Adrian said. 'I'll tell him today.'

'Just so we're clear – what exactly will you tell him?'

'I'll tell him about Tammy. I'll invite him round to the flat.'

She was shaking her head. She smiled but it was a perplexed, enquiring sort of a smile. 'You don't *invite* him round to your flat. You do see that, don't you? He's not your *guest*. I mean, if you give Tammy the opportunity, I'm sure she'll make a fantastic stepmother. People speak very highly of her you know.' Adrian's face must have registered his confusion but Harriet was now looking across at him in the same bright, placid way, as though she were offering him reassurance, as though she were saying: This is where we are now. This is what we now are.

A slender, moving presence in the hallway, the click of the latch. Oliver: his small ten-year-old self, all that remarkable, unknowing beauty.

'What are you two doing out here?' he said. 'It's freezing.'

'Just catching up, Ol,' Adrian said. 'Everything all right?' He gave Oliver's shoulder a small pat.

'Why you wearing that?' Oliver said. He gave the jacket's wide sleeve an unhappy little tug.

'I was just about to head in,' Harriet said.

'We going now, then?'

'That's the plan,' Adrian said. 'Michael thinks it's going to rain. Is that coat waterproof?'

'Michael's weird.'

'Oliver!' Harriet said. She stepped back into the house, turning a frown towards him as she passed him in the hallway. 'I'll see you later,' she said. 'In a better mood, hopefully.'

'Laters, *Mom*,' Oliver said.

*

'New handset?' Adrian asked. They were stuck on the South Circular, next to the cricket club, not far from Sydenham Woods.

Oliver tapped in a code. 'Mum's old one.'

'Mum's given you a phone?'

'What's wrong with that?' His expert fingers were deleting long chains of photographs. 'I was one of the last people in Year 6 to get one.'

'They backed up?'

'Dunno,' Oliver said. The images – one of him smiling, one of him playing football on the Astroturf – vanishing into rapid motionful whiteness.

'Those saved somewhere else?'

'Chill, Dad,' Oliver said.

He sat himself further back into his seat, stretching his legs out before planting his shoes onto the dashboard. Adrian wanted to tell him to put his feet down. He'd never found any of it easy, all those times he'd had to ask Oliver to perform some basic function, to get dressed or to brush his teeth, his voice an airless, wandering sound, a series of unfocused complaints eventually rising to a comically infuriated pitch. He knew even as it was happening that the anger was mostly with himself, at his curious impotence, at that shadowy feeling he'd always had of existing apart from the principle rules and mechanisms of the home. At work it was as if everything were reversed. He enjoyed the modest power, taking decisions, the adrenalin of confrontation and risk. If he'd had a few drinks, he'd get carried away with himself and he'd say things like 'theory is the enemy of action'. He'd started becoming high-minded about people who didn't *commit*, who didn't just *get on and do it*. He recognised the irony. It felt like someone was playing a trick on him, teaching him some rudimentary moral lesson.

The traffic had come to a stop. Oliver was still deleting photographs, the same thin, singular attentiveness. Videos too: footage of that carol concert. They'd been living apart by then, but Harriet had thought they should go together. She'd filmed the whole thing. The vivid entreaties of the teacher leading the singing, the kids' tremulous, winsome voices. 'I enjoyed that concert,' Adrian said.

'Creating more memory,' Oliver said. A horn sounded. Another sounded back. 'So I can download Minecraft.'

'You allowed the phone all the time? What about homework?'

'What about it? Mum's stopped giving me a hard time about that sort of stuff, just so you know.'

'Has she?'

'Mum's much more relaxed than she used to be,' Oliver said. 'It's because of Matthias,' he said after a moment or two.

'Who's Matthias?'

'Mum's therapist.' Oliver uncrossed his legs but his feet stayed where they were, raised up on the dashboard. Adrian noticed a distant rumbling anger moving closer. 'You're doing that drumming thing, Dad . . . with your fingers,' Oliver said.

Adrian stilled his fingers, tightening them around the wheel. 'Why don't we do some maths together, then?'

'Who actually records an entire hour-long carol concert?' Oliver said. He adjusted the volume on his phone. They both stared at the red-jumpered kids, the soloist who was taking her turn at the front. *I had a dream that I was standing on a hillside, And all the lights of town were shining far below*. 'She's got a good voice, hasn't she?' Adrian said. 'She in your year?'

'Year 4,' Oliver said.

Adrian remembered Harriet sitting upright on the pew in the church, the tightly wound stiffness. And afterwards the dismal silence until they'd found Oliver in the car park, standing together in a lifeless three in the middle of all the other children and parents. He remembered the feeling of exposure, of sensing people looking at him. Harriet would have accused him of vanity or paranoia but he wasn't so sure. Some of the mums knew Tammy. One or two of them had known about it all before Harriet found out. He remembered trying to strike up a conversation with Oliver but it had felt so fitful and hard. The difficulty of talking to his own flesh and blood struck him as another apt punishment, another strange reversal. He and Tammy could talk for hours. They talked about everything – difficult things. Those long weekends in bed, finally pulling up the blinds at dusk. She was so entirely open to him. If she wanted something, she told him what she wanted. She directed him in the simplest, plainest English. Where to put his hands. Precisely what to do with them. How the thing he was doing made her feel. If she was embarrassed, or excited, she flushed. If she was sad, she said she was sad. If she wanted to show love, she touched him in a particular way or told him so in words. Sometimes he struggled to comprehend the simplicity of it all – that all this happy, mutual pleasure could be as forthcoming and reliable as it was. He thought about leaving her that morning, the sensation of her body surrounding his. He could still hear her wordless exhortations, still see the rising journey marked out on her face, her disbelief at the exquisite material generosity of physical pleasure.

The cars. A lengthy, bulky, unwieldy circuit. Oliver too,

somehow part of this other world. His legs replaced into the footwell, his slender body slouched forwards, the phone a lustrous link between one hand and the next. The concert was gone now. The photographs too – the one of him smiling, the one of him on the Astroturf.

'You hungry?' Adrian said. 'What do you feel like? Pizza?'

'A burger would be good,' Oliver said.

'A burger it is,' Adrian said.

It was a place they hadn't come to before, but it was a place they came to now. Adrian liked the emptiness. He liked ordering at the counter. The food came fast. There were friendly little distractions for Oliver, too: a soft-drinks machine with its own frothy dispensing gun. Free refills of Coke and Fanta and Sprite, and even a button that ground out chunky blocks of ice. The burgers came wrapped up in plain brown paper, and the brown paper bags of salty chips were always generously overfilled. Adrian drank his coffee. He thought it might help. He thought it might clear his head. He was formulating silently. There's something I'd like to talk to you about, Oliver. There's something I've been meaning to have a chat to you about. I've met someone, Ol. Her name's Tammy. Tam. You'll like her. She's nice. His heart lurched this way and that, idiotically. He was losing any sense of proportion, of how difficult or not this all was, of what any of it meant. A waitress delivered their order on a tray. The restaurants had been started up by a father and his four sons who'd blind-tasted all the ingredients before they'd found out what the ingredients cost. There were American newspaper articles celebrating the family's success.

'This looks all right, doesn't it, Ol? Do you want ketchup or anything?'

'Yes, please,' Oliver said.

Adrian stood up from the table and went over to the serving station with the large vats of tomato ketchup and mayonnaise and bright yellow mustard. He'd brought a napkin with him, and he siphoned off the sauces, wondering if he should have asked for a plate instead.

'There we go!' he said. He laid the napkin down cautiously onto the table. 'Chips?'

Oliver's hands delved into the bag. 'These are good,' he said.

'How's the milkshake?'

'Good,' Oliver said.

'How's football?' Adrian reached for his coffee.

'We won seven-nil last week.'

'Great news!'

'I barely got a touch.'

'Doesn't Mr Noble give you a go up front if you're winning?'

'If you're a defender you're a defender. And I'm definitely a defender . . .' He helped himself to more chips. 'Thinking of giving it up anyway.'

'I thought you loved football.'

'Did you?' Oliver said. He slid the phone from his pocket and he placed it onto the table. He spun it around and around like a pointer on a game-board. 'Know Mum's login?' he asked. Adrian gave his head a small shake. He remembered every single one of Harriet's passwords, but why did he feel he shouldn't remember them, that to admit to being in possession of that knowledge wasn't allowed? 'I'm going to download two new games when we get back.'

'I thought we'd go to the park after lunch,' Adrian said. 'Have a run around. That sound good?'

'It's going to rain, isn't it?' Oliver said. He'd finished with the bag of chips and he shoved it to one side of the table. 'You ever played Minecraft? You can build *literally* anything. Like, I mean, *literally* anything. There's nothing in this world that's not in that world.' His face brightened. 'Say something, Dad. Anything. Like any word. Any word that comes into your head.'

'Chips,' Adrian said.

'Do potatoes count? Minecraft's got tonnes of potatoes. Think of something else.'

'A palm tree?'

'You can pretty much spawn any kind of tree. Think of something else – something even rarer than a palm tree.'

'What about birds? What about a golden eagle?'

'Minecraft's got every type of eagle there is,' Oliver said. 'They have this high-pitched squawk like real eagles do. Fergus and me built this really cool structure and we put loads of different birds in there and we fed them seeds and stuff. Guess what? Fergus is even allowed to play Fortnite at weekends now. Mum said she'd think about getting it for me for my birthday.' He offered Adrian the remainder of the milkshake. 'Wanna try?'

'I'm good, Ol,' Adrian said.

'Hey – that reminds me. What are *you* getting me? For my birthday, I mean. I've got a list.'

'You keep this car tidy, don't you?' Oliver said. The rain was falling hard and without pattern onto the windscreen. It was

November but there were still some browning leaves on the trees, some now in flight or descent, disturbed by the wintery gusts. The sky was mostly a heavy passage of grey except for where the clouds had thinned into a milkier, yellower veil. 'Smells nice, too,' Oliver said. Adrian thought about that constant terrible messiness of their old car. Neither of them had bothered to clear it out: the stale crisps in the footwells, the babygrows and stripey dungarees intended for charity shops strewn around the boot. It had become a point of principle to look after this one. Tammy had one of those hand-held hoovers which made everything easy; it fitted neatly into its special holder next to the fridge. Of course, it had already occurred to him that it was a banal form of atonement. The furtive trip to Cargiant with the new Visa card he'd kept hidden in a drawer at work. The furtive trips to Tammy's flat or, when he couldn't wait any longer, picking her up from that bus stop, the coarse and heavy weight of the picnic rug on top of them, the awful pleasure of the lovemaking on that silent street in Beckenham near the golf course. The grand, well-lit houses set back from the road, the oval lawns and the yew trees, the odd passing car. 'You like it when people drive past us, don't you?' Tammy had said. She was like that: the occasional light-handed ability to shock.

'Basically, Dad, you can get any kind of bird,' Oliver was saying. 'You can get flamingos. You can get peacocks. *Literally* any species. And they all have different sorts of cries. They even lay eggs! And the tame ones come and sit on your shoulder!' Adrian made a cursory reply. He'd noticed this before: how functional his role in these conversations could become. He wondered if Oliver noticed it too. He thought about Tammy, how just lying there with her on the sofa stirred something in him every night, how the simple act of bringing her into his imagination could unify every stray thought, every stray part of him into a dense, singular impulse, its trajectory so wholly defined. As if the present were already in some kind of terrible forward motion. He remembered conversations he'd had with old friends, the crass jokes after a few drinks – the words people used and the laughter that followed all seemed so entirely distinct from the reality of any of it. There'd been others before Tammy: the girl he'd met in that bar in Madrid, the temp he'd kissed in the basement at work. Just thinking about them, remembering them, opened him up to that same unyielding energy. A pure and complete distillation of something. But what? Where did any of it lead? The dragging, insular sadness afterwards. The soft nub of guilt.

They were at the traffic lights next to the closed-down Harvester. There were posters advertising a circus which had been torn off in strips from a wall. Adrian listened to the rain hitting the car, the churn of the wipers, the sound of the rubber pulling against the glass. Oliver's head was lowered, the frame of his body still slouched forwards. The phone was on his lap, that radiant centre. Adrian knew the answer to the question was sitting there, right next to him. And sometimes it did make perfect sense: the love for a child so deeply weighted. But there were other times when the scope of those feelings eluded him, when the Saturday mornings wore him down, when he was unable to plumb those wells of feeling – the deep, quiet wells so strangely counter to the exhilaration and heady joy he experienced with Tammy. With the others. With Harriet too, a long time ago. He looked through the rainy glass to his right. He could see a row of fir trees, a gate, the

166

path behind it leading up to the woods. He imagined himself abandoning the car, walking out across the traffic, following the path. 'How about coming over to my flat next weekend?' he said. 'I've got it all a bit more sorted now.'

'Sure,' Oliver said.

'I'd like you to meet someone, too,' Adrian said.

Oliver repositioned himself in his seat. He seemed to be holding himself up now. There seemed to be a broadening of his shoulders. 'I was wondering when you were going to mention *the girlfriend*,' he said.

'Tammy,' Adrian said.

'I know her name, Dad.'

'You do?'

'I actually think it's a really good thing,' Oliver said. 'Like . . . Mum's totally moved on. It's not like it used to be. At the beginning.' He wove his fingers together, stretching the clasped hands into the air in front of him. 'I'm sure she's really nice.'

They were on either end of the sofa. Harriet was wearing a pair of tight, black jeans. Adrian could see the striped T-shirt she liked wearing in summer under her jumper. He could make out a silver necklace, too. She hadn't worn jewellery before. He wondered briefly whether someone had given the necklace to her. Oliver was up in his room finishing off his homework. Adrian had carried an extra chair up the staircase, placing it next to the one sitting at the desk. They could see the tops of trees through the Velux windows. The large pine looked woeful and ragged. The sparser, nearly leafless crowns of others seemed oddly robust. They could see red chimney stacks, seagulls circling the air in threes or fours. There had

167

been no complaining from Oliver. He'd answered the ten questions on fractions, rushing a little, like he usually did. The numbers he'd written down weren't minute or illegible. They'd seemed to Adrian a normal size. He'd sat next to his son, watching the drifts of clouds, the dark umbrous banks, the softer, lighter openings, and he'd said to himself, everything is a phase. We move through phases. He'd felt more peaceful than he'd felt in a long time.

He felt peaceful now, too, sitting on his end of the sofa, a glass of wine in his hand. Harriet had tucked her legs neatly under herself. She was wearing thin, nylon socks.

'I'm really proud of you, Ade,' she said. 'I'll be honest with you – I didn't think you'd do it.'

'It just sort of came out,' Adrian said. 'While we were in the car.' He took a sip from his glass. 'How do you think he knew?'

'No idea! I promise you – I haven't breathed a word. And he really did seem genuinely fine?'

'He really did,' Adrian said. He tilted the glass towards her. 'Testament to you.'

'Matthias talks a lot about "rupture and repair". I find it a consoling thought.' She picked up her glass. Her gaze shifted away from his face. 'I don't think I would have met Sam if I hadn't had therapy. Does that make sense?' She moved her feet out from under herself and she stretched her legs along the length of the sofa. 'Sorry – I wasn't sure I was going to say anything, but somehow it feels right. Telling you now.'

Adrian experienced a hard, painful lurch in his stomach. 'How long have you been seeing each other?' he said.

'A few months now.' Harriet was smiling at him in the same benevolent way she'd smiled at him on the doorstep that morning. 'You'll like him. Oliver likes him.'

Adrian wasn't thinking clearly. He was aware of that. And he was aware how jealous he felt, how terrified. One of her feet was balanced on the other in a pose that might have suggested friendliness or flirtation or indifference, he wasn't sure. He lifted the nearest one into his hands. He was sweating. He pressed his thumbs onto her heel, onto the arch of her foot. She closed her eyes. 'I remember these,' she said. They both heard it then: the downward charge of steps on the stairs. The door banging open with the same urgent rush. For a brief second the impression of the scene registered as a shadowing on the boy's face. Adrian got up quickly from the sofa. His shoe knocked into his glass of wine. 'Fuck,' he said.

'Shit! Where's the salt?' Harriet said.

'Will you come and see something, Dad? Before you go? Those burgers were amazing, weren't they? Shall we go back there next weekend?' Oliver signalled impatiently with his hand. 'Come on! I want to show you this like really *amazing* thing. I've built a portal! D'you know what portals are? You know how I was telling you all about spawning. How you spawn *everything*. Basically you build a portal out of obsidian – that's a type of rock – and then you can travel between the Overworld and the Nether. The Overworld is where you start off – like here, basically – but the Nether is different. The Nether's like a ginormous cave. There's no daylight. No weather or anything. The only things that grow are these massive fungi and the only light is the light generated by the portals or by lava or by fire . . . but you have to create those . . .'

Harriet walked back through the door carrying a bottle of stain remover. The same pink bottle lived under Tammy's

169

sink. 'This stuff's amazing,' she said. 'Loads better than salt!'

'Let me,' Adrian said. He knelt down next to her on the carpet.

'Dad! Seriously! You have to come and see this world!' Oliver said but he was also watching them kneeling over the stain.

Harriet started spraying the whitish liquid. It bubbled and frothed. 'Honestly, Ade, it's fine.'

'Dad! Please come. *Please!*'

'Let me just give Mum a hand with this, Ol,' Adrian said. 'I'll be up in two minutes.'

The boy started counting. 'One, two three . . .' He wandered out of the room. 'Four, five, six, seven, eight . . .'

Harriet stood up. Adrian was still kneeling on the carpet so she offered him her hand. The benign expression had gone. 'Come here, you idiot,' she said. She held onto him and he laid his head down onto her shoulder. His cheek rested against the fine links of the new necklace. She tightened her grip on his waist and she held his head close. She spoke to him soothingly, the same way she might have spoken to Oliver after a fall. Blood on his knees. A thin layer of skin coming away from his palm. 'Time's up, Dad!' a voice called down. 'Come here now and see this *world*!'

Our Name Means Unique

Madeleine Dunnigan

Mushrooms are in season. I get up early one bright October morning and go to the forest near my home to gather them. *Little pig*, my sister teased me years ago, *sniffing them out*. Back then, I was the only one, but mushrooms have become popular so there are lots of little pigs in the forest this morning. I hate the ones my age most: tall and tastefully dressed, with special gloves and a child or two. Stamping around and letting their dogs shit everywhere. Even so, they don't know the best places to look, under moist folds of leaves and gnarled roots. As I go deeper into the forest a dog follows me, a chocolate-brown tuxedo. I bend down and feel the heat of his small body, which is shaking slightly. Then he is gone, running stupidly. I do not like dogs; I also dislike coffee, shoes indoors and Dido. I like heavy-bottomed pans, butter and the Amalfi Coast, although I have never been there. I find a kind of peace this morning, with the pale sunlight that slices the forest floor, and the snatches of blue above that make the naked branches look darker. As I dig and gather and scrape, I think of how suddenly mushrooms appear, as if from nowhere. But, in fact, they have been growing for many years beneath the ground, threadlike bodies that hold each other

171

in a taut web. Invisible yet potent. If you have ever picked mushrooms before, you will know how careful you need to be. I think of the magic held in these muddy things, poison and cure, nourishment and pleasure, and I smile to myself.

Tonight, I am cooking Friday-night dinner for my family and it needs to be very special. Shabbat must always be special. I have not seen much of my parents since The Incident – even less of my sister. They paid for a therapist and a flat. *Independence is what she needs*, my mother said. *After all, she is over thirty. And space*, she said as she turned away. *Space is what we need.* I have spent the past year alone, thinking. Talking to my therapist. Reading. Understanding how the world works – how we form constellations with others, those bonds between us making a pattern, which repeats over and over. And working out how to break that pattern.

At first, my parents were reluctant to come – *That sounds like a lot of pressure, darling* – but when I told them my therapist said it was a good idea, they agreed. *I'm so glad you're talking to someone*, my mother said. Persuading my sister was harder. I told her I missed her – like before. *I miss us the way we were before.* She softened. My sister can't resist flattery; it is one of her best and worst traits. I also said she could bring Frank. She was surprised that I knew his name. I told her our mother had filled me in on her new man and that to be honest I didn't care either way, I just thought she might like to. That clinched it.

Family is very important. *It is important*, my mother says, *to be together*.

Thinking about my sister and about The Incident makes my stomach hurt so I pour myself another glass of wine, finishing the bottle. My parents arrive arguing. They pause momentarily to greet me: my mother hesitates before kissing me on the cheek, my father pats my head. Then they continue. My father had tried and failed to change the halogen light bulb in their living-room reading lamp.

'All I wanted,' my mother says as she dips a hummus chip in home-made tapenade, 'all I wanted, was to have a cup of tea and a bit of peace and quiet. I was so looking forward to reading. To stopping. For a moment.'

'I've just finished reading *Hitler*. One thousand pages on the man. My studies on the Holocaust are complete,' my father says and leans back in his chair.

'I'm going to live alone,' my mother announces. 'I am. I'm going to get a divorce.'

I open a fresh bottle of wine and pour them each a glass. Neither of my parents are big drinkers.

'Put it in the recycling at least,' my mother says, holding up the empty bottle of Stellenbosch that was standing next to where I am cooking.

'Don't be so judgemental,' I reply. But really, this is a good sign: it shows she is relaxed.

'*The Rise and Fall of the Third Reich*, *Hitler*, all of Hannah Arendt,' my father continues. 'Did you know that Hannah Arendt blames the Jews for anti-Semitism? It comes from a sense they have that they're somehow *special*.'

'I think that was the view that made her rather unpopular,' my mother says, not looking up from the copy of *Feast* she is flicking through. 'Is this what you're making, darling?'

'Why?'

I have already begun to fry the mushrooms. It is tempting, when frying mushrooms, to add too much fat, initially. The turgid vegetables guzzle it up and remain stiff and unyielding. But sweat them long enough and eventually they give up, weeping into the pan.

'Mushroom risotto. It's just a bit . . . well . . . you know.'

'It's seasonal,' I say.

My mother holds up her hands and widens her eyes and I remind myself to be good. I do not like criticism; it is something I have always struggled to accept. So my mother would say to the grim-faced teachers who told me not to return to school. Later, after I had filed away my drawings, the drawings I had completed in painstaking detail but which apparently were 'not appropriate' for children my age, when I lay in bed, face to pillow, my mother rubbed my back and said that I was special, *Our name means unique in German*, and that I would, one day, do something spectacular. Now, I imagine picking up the empty wine bottle and smashing it on the counter. I imagine the relief it will give me, like after urinating.

Instead, I say, 'I picked the mushrooms myself, Mama.'

'How lovely, darling, that is so clever of you, isn't it?' She hits my father on the arm. 'We're just *so* happy you're – You look *marvellous*. It's lovely to all be together, isn't it?' She hits my father again.

There is a silence. I am not about to break it. I am chopping garlic. Then my father says, 'Did you see there was an exhibition on mushrooms at that big gallery in town?'

'I can't take you anywhere, honestly,' my mother says. 'I'd be better off alone.'

My mother threatens to divorce my father every couple of hours. They have been married for over thirty years.

My mother comes over to me. I am stirring the risotto

rice and adding small amounts of white wine.

'How are you doing, darling?' As she talks, she reaches for the wooden spoon I am using.

'Fine.' I stir in the opposite direction, confusing her.

She steps back to look at me. 'I mean, is everything OK, since – We've been worried. We wanted to give you space. Space is so important.' I say nothing. 'To heal.'

My mother is fit and healthy. Yes, she dyes her hair, but her biceps are her own, so are her abs, as is the radiance that shines from her unblemished, successful face. She is smaller than me, though, which gives me a little satisfaction. Standing in front of her now, the risotto pan steaming between us, I have the overwhelming desire to fold myself into her, like the old days, but I remember what my therapist said earlier this week, *Powerful actions need not be big ones*, and continue to stir the rice.

'Of course we're OK, Mama.'

At that moment, the doorbell rings.

My sister is ten years younger than me – *our accidental angel* – and she is utterly and uncompromisingly gorgeous. Small like my mother, with a figure like Marilyn Monroe. She has these curls that tumble down her back, hooking and spilling over one another. She has, like the rest of us, the family schnoz, but when she smiles the most adorable little crinkles form around the bridge and at the sides of her eyes so she looks truly happy. When we were younger, we were inseparable. A smaller version of me but more brilliant, she clung to my side and followed me around. I was God; my sister, an angel. She was no accident: she is my breath, my brain, my beating heart.

My stomach flips as she enters the room. I finish my

glass of wine. This must be Frank behind her. Worse than I expected. My mother told me there was an age difference. Frank is, after all, her university professor. But this man, he is – long hair, colourful T-shirt and large trainers – pathetic in that particular way only older men are.

Frank does not know about The Incident and, *In any case*, my mother said on the phone before agreeing to this dinner, *it did not happen*. My therapist says it will take time for everyone to understand; that we each see the world in a different way. We each have our own triggers. Music while eating, frayed toothbrushes, queues. *Families*, she said, *are complicated*.

'What's that smell?' my sister says. Frank holds out a bottle – something cheap by the look of it.

'Thanks, Frank,' I say in my sweetest voice and smile.

My mother sighs. 'God, the money I spent on those teeth!'

I did not wear my retainer post-braces and my teeth are very crooked. My mother frowns every time I smile. My sister has perfect teeth.

'You've got lipstick on your teeth,' my sister says and walks past me.

I grip the bottle tighter.

Before tonight – before The Incident, even – when we still lived together, my sister would creep into my room at night and curl up with me. *Stop watching that trash*, she teased as I stared at Carrie Bradshaw's tiny frame in a pink cropped shirt that didn't cover her bra and a green belt over her bare, flat midriff. My sister would close the laptop and stroke my damp cheeks. Later, when she slipped out of bed, her silhouette was like a ripple at night, moonlight glancing off her shoulder, her hip, the dimples at the base of her back.

'Smells delicious,' Frank says, adjusting his orange laces.

'We can't stay long,' my sister says.

My sister is wearing something uncharacteristically drab – a shirt that makes her look like a giant napkin. My sister is usually very glamorous. She wears silk wrap dresses, gold bangles and beaded earrings that get caught in her hair. She wears lipstick: my favourite is a nude called taupe that is only just darker than her olive skin. Now, I rub the same shade off my own lips with the back of my hand.

'What kind of mushrooms did you pick?' my mother asks.

'Did you hear about the party in Italy?' my father interrupts. 'Went foraging for rhubarb.'

'Dad, please! Not another lecture.' My sister has her head in her hands.

My sister looks like she is about to vomit. I want to go to her and kiss her forehead, the soft bit where her angel hairs curl. Then I see my mother's face, a curious smile playing across it. I look at my sister once again. The big shirt billowing out in front, the just perceptible bulge. And I am caught. I do not know what to do.

It makes a difference to the plan, a sixth person. It has always given me trouble, people not doing what they are supposed to do. People moving out of place. That is probably why my mother did not tell me that my sister is pregnant. Why she asks me if I am *OK*, while holding me at arm's length. Why I am alone.

My mother sits by my sister, her arm tight around her. '*Darling*,' she says. I cannot go to them, stranded on the other side of the kitchen island, closed off from their embrace. I grip the risotto spoon and make lists in my head. *Cortinarius rubellus, Amanita phalloides, Galerina marginata,* my second favourite. In the medieval era people associated mushrooms with melancholy because of their earthiness and moisture.

'*Darling,*' my mother says again. 'Did you get those vitamins I sent you? You must take them every day. They're very expensive.'

'*Excuse me,* I was in the middle of telling a story. So, these foragers in Italy found what they thought was rhubarb and picked the lot,' my father says. 'Went home and made a pie –'

'Crumble,' my mother says. 'No one makes rhubarb pie.'

'Wouldn't it have been a tart if they were Italian?' My sister looks up.

'Yes, I think it would probably be something with frangipane, since it's Europe,' says Frank.

'*Please,*' my father says. 'So they made this rhubarb *whatever,* and started feeling a bit queasy.'

'But it *matters,*' my mother says. 'The details of your story matter. Why rhubarb? Why pie? We need to *believe* in the details in order for it to work.'

'I'm trying to tell you –'

'Can't get any signal,' Frank says, looking at his phone, 'but I'm pretty sure the Italians would have made a tart.'

'Actually, Mum, they're way more likely to make a pie than crumble. What's more English than a crumble?' my sister says.

'Oh, darling, I don't know about these things. The day you come to me as an expert on the English is the day I die.' My mother, born in London, daughter of a Jewish refugee and an unknown Spanish bartender, is adamant that she is European. 'But, darling, are you getting enough sleep? Sleep is key.'

My sister hasn't looked at me for several minutes. 'We know the sex,' she says quietly. 'A little girl.' The way she pulls at her cuticle tells me she is nervous.

I look at my hands, gripping the wooden spoon, black slimy things in the pan. Years ago, my mother bought me a set of good heavy-bottomed pans. I like pans because they are simple: they have a function and a purpose. I love the set of Le Creuset pans my mother bought me because they are reliable and heavy and a measure of my strength: I used to need two hands to lift a pan, now I only need one. I used to wonder if, in another life, I could have done something like been a blacksmith, but when I told my mother she scoffed and said, *Darling*. The risotto is sticking. I start stirring again, counting each rotation in my head.

'A girl!' my mother squeals. 'A girl means slow sperm. Catch up, Frank.'

Frank chokes on his wine.

My mother is a sex therapist. When I was four, I was sent out of class for explaining to my peer group how heterosexual penetrative intercourse works; my mother had a fight with the teacher when she picked me up. In my bedroom was a poster of the female and male genitalia and by six I could name each part. I learnt the female pudendum – *mons pubis, labia majora, labia minora, vestibule of the vagina, bulb of the vestibule, greater and lesser vestibular glands* and *vaginal orifice* – by singing it, like plainsong. My mother laughed, *Naughty monk*. I was less interested in the male genitalia, perhaps because I didn't have any, so I covered that half of the poster with a print-out of Enya. When I hit puberty, I developed an enlarged Venus mount, which was why my pubis looked like the bulge of a boy in my PE shorts. But when I shouted this back to Robbie Millen, he just laughed along with everyone else. It didn't help that I was large all over, round and soft like a bread roll. I still wonder what it would be like to slice Robbie Millen's knees off. The one thing I remember from the male genitalia is the pouch of Douglas: a cul-de-sac between the rectum and urinary bladder that collects extra fluids like blood and pus. It is also where tumours can develop. Women have one too, but we also have the uterus, where we make life.

'*Mum*, we've *talked* about this,' my sister says. I see her reach under the table towards Frank. My heart tightens. My sister is young, barely in her twenties, still basically a child. Too young to form significant and meaningful bonds with anyone – anyone else – and certainly too young to have a baby.

While my mother worked on her career and my father read his books, I raised my sister. I bathed her and untangled her unruly hair. I made her dinner, a mountain of chips rising from a lake of peas, with fish-finger monsters. I taught her to read; first, through the posters my mother had bought me, and later, through the books I discovered alone – Italo Calvino, Shirley Jackson, Philippa Pearce, worlds that we could dive into and make our own. After I left school for the final time, after the thing with Robbie Millen and the hammer, she held my hand and told me she loved me no matter what. And later, when I had one of my episodes on the street, she snarled at people who stared and shouted at those who called me names.

She looked after me as much as I looked after her, and that love spilled over. In bed, I put my arms around her, she ran her finger along my collarbone, I touched her shoulder, she, my rib cage, our hands moving in synchronicity. We looked at the poster on my wall and whispered parts of ourselves in each other's ears like a spell.

Then my sister stopped speaking to me, stopped looking me in the eye. When she passed me on the stairs, she whispered *Forget*. When I returned home one day, she stood in the corner crying while my mother followed me through the house screaming words like *grooming* and *responsibility* and *fucking shitshow*. I became a little overwhelmed. I smashed things: candlesticks, ramekins, vases. Anything made of glass and which made a noise. It felt good. I have spoken to my therapist about this moment and this – this smashing – is what my therapist calls The Incident. She says I should trust my instincts more, before they become overwhelming. But I have not spoken to her about the before. When we lay, my sister and I, tangled together, looking at the glow in the dark stars on my ceiling. I have not, like my sister, given that part of us away – to anyone.

Now my sister is pregnant and I do not know what to do.

'A toast!' my father says. 'To the wee bairn! Look, can I finish –'
    'Food's ready!'
I serve at the counter, filling the blue-glazed plates with hot, sticky rice. As I shape it into perfect mounds, I realise what I must do; I suppose I've known it all along. I feel disappointed that I won't get the ending I had planned, but I also feel proud for coming to this conclusion without breaking anything. I dribble some truffle oil and a shaving,

181

thin as skin, of Parmesan.

'Have you read that new book on mushrooms?' Frank says. 'By Casper someone –'

'Yes,' I say. 'It's shit.'

I think about my funeral often. Hundreds of mourners there all prostrate with grief, Enya playing as my coffin is brought in. Better yet, a terrible accident in which I am maimed or hurt in some way and everyone flocks to me, full of sympathy and outrage. Me, benevolent and stunning in a wheelchair.

I watch as each of my family and Frank take a tentative mouthful and I watch as the relief spreads across their faces.

'It's delicious,' my mother says. 'Really, I am so impressed with how *far* you've come, darling.'

My sister looks at me and, for the first time in over a year, she smiles. My heart soars and I wonder if I have made the right decision. If, once they have gone, I will be able to bear the silence once again. My father clears a tickle in the back of his throat. Then my mother fans herself. 'A little hot flush.'

'What happened in the story, Dad?'

'Ah, well, they started to feel a bit queasy after this rhubarb *thing* and' – he coughs – 'one by one, they dropped down. Turns out they'd picked the stems of young hemlock.' He manages to finish before breaking into a coughing fit. My mother flocks to him.

'Chard,' I say.

'What?' my sister says.

My father is spluttering now, unable to breathe.

'Could someone get him a glass of water for God's sake!' My mother's voice is tinged with panic. Frank runs to the sink.

'Rhubarb looks nothing like hemlock,' I say. 'It would have been chard.'

As my father turns a most startling shade of pink, gasping, my mother whacks him on the back, in one strong, heavy movement, and a small piece of mushroom flies through the air. My father takes a deep breath, my mother sits back down, Frank stands by the table, glass of water in hand. I feel the glow of everyone's eyes on me.

'That settles it, then,' my mother says. 'They would have made a quiche.'

We finish our plates in silence. Frank compliments the food and I think he is about to ask for more, but then my sister puts a hand on his arm, gesturing with her head. My mother offers to drive them. She pecks me on the cheek and tells me 'How lovely it is to be all together again.' My father puts a hand on my arm as he walks past. Frank gives me a wave from the door and my sister looks at me, and nods. And very suddenly, they are gone.

I feel in my pocket, where I keep a small, moist mushroom. The mushroom I had planned to sprinkle on each person's plate, but which I decided to keep. My favourite mushroom of all, *Amanita virosa*: Destroying Angel.

I think about what happened, what could have and what still might. My mother at one end of the table, my father next to her. My sister opposite him and next to Frank. *Don't you look beautiful*, my mother says, pointing at me. *Make room for our daughter, our most precious and beloved. A toast!* my father says. *Make room for your sister, let her sit down. To the only one we love*, my sister smiles, babe in one arm, standing graciously and passing me the small infant, *to our one true* love. *To family!* they cry in unison. *To being together!* And me, sitting at the head of the table, adored and adorned, truly beloved.

Because, you see, in some ways, it is *our* child – my sister's and mine. The consequence of a series of events triggered by and born out of our love. It is a sign: the beginning of our own, our new, family. The constellation expands, the web tightens, and the many possibilities of life spread out before me, a never-ending spool of maybes and might bes. I feel my magic grow.

Contributors' Bios

Madeleine Dunnigan is a writer living in London. Her fiction and non-fiction have been published by *Momaya Short Story Review*, *Patterned Ground* and *3:AM Magazine*. She is currently completing a master's in creative and life writing at Goldsmiths, where she was awarded the Isaac Arthur Green Fellowship. She is part of the inaugural Genesis Jewish Book Week Emerging Writers' Programme and is working on her first novel.

Kate Ellis is a writer and ex-bookseller based in London. Her short fiction has been published in the *Open Pen Anthology*, *The Mechanics' Institute Review* and *The London Short Story Prize Anthology* among others. In 2020, she was longlisted for the Deborah Rogers Foundation Award for her debut novel. She runs the Brick Lane Bookshop Short Story Prize. Twitter: @katesmalleyelli

Katherine Gutierrez's writing has been featured in *Breakwater Review* as a 2020 Fiction Contest longlistee, as Editor's Choice for Fincham Press anthology *Purple Lights*, and was awarded the John Hopkins Poetry Prize. She is currently working on a short-story collection and resides in Kent, England.

Kate Horsley's short stories have appeared in the *Brixton Review of Books* and the *Observer*. She teaches contemporary British literature at Boston University, and is writing her first novel.

Aoife Inman is a writer from the Lizard Peninsula, Cornwall. Her short fiction has been published in *The London Magazine*, shortlisted for the V. S. Pritchett Prize and won the 2018 Ryedale Book Festival Short Story Competition. She has an MA in history from the University of Manchester, where her research focused on the relationship between memory and landscape.

Aden Jamal is a pseudonymous British writer. Born and raised in the melting pot of London, where mansions regularly sit beside council estates, he's naturally drawn to contradictions, rudeness and overpaying for *everything*. His writing typically explores the multi-faceted Black British reality of this messy country and probes the universal gap between expectation and desire.

Ramya Jegatheesan was born to Sri Lankan Tamil parents and lives in London. Her short stories can be found in the 2015 UCL Publishers' Prize anthology, *Untitled: Voices* and *REWRITE READS*. She was shortlisted for the 2020 Lost the Plot Work in Progress Prize and is a writer on Hachette's Grow Your Story programme. She is a Curtis Brown Creative alumna.

Cllr Dr **Denise Jones**, HonDLitt, FRSA, Freeman of the City of London, studied graphic design, was a primary school teacher and has worked with the bookshop that she co-founded since 1978. She lives in Cable Street and is an elected Labour councillor in Tower Hamlets. Denise strongly supports the arts and is a board member of Rich Mix, the V&A Museum of Childhood, Trinity Buoy Wharf Trust, Create London, Aldgate & Allhallows Foundation, Mulberry Schools Trust, The Portal Trust and Lee Valley Regional Park Authority.

Nicholas Kemp is a secondary school English teacher from London. He has a master's in Renaissance literature and is a student at the Curtis Brown Creative Writing School. He is writing *The Body Beautiful*, a novel about bodybuilding and body dysmorphia; 'Deadlifting' is taken from the opening of the novel.

Leeor Ohayon is a writer from London based in Norwich. He is currently enrolled on the MA Creative Writing Prose Fiction at the University of East Anglia, where he is working on a collection of short stories. Leeor's short story 'bedbugs' took first place in the Leicester Writes Short Story Prize 2021, and he has had a number of non-fiction articles published on online platforms such as *+972*, *Vittles* and *Vashti*, among others.

JP Pangilinan-O'Brien is a teacher from West London. He is currently working on a collection of connected short stories, which explores questions of identity, belonging and diaspora.

Aisha Phoenix's collection, *Bat Monkey and Other Stories*, was shortlisted for the 2020 SI Leeds Literary Prize. Her work has appeared in Inkandescent's *Mainstream* anthology; Peepal Tree Press's *Filigree*; the 2020 National Flash Fiction

Day anthology, *Root, Branch, Tree*; the Bath Flash Fiction anthology Volume Two, *The Lobsters Run Free*; *Strange Horizons*; *Litro USA Online*; and *The Mechanics' Institute Review Online*. Twitter: @FirebirdN4

Danielle Vrublevskis was born in Germany, grew up in Bristol and now lives in London. She's worked as a researcher, bookseller and translator, both in the UK and abroad. Her work has previously been shortlisted for the Bristol Short Story Prize.

Nayela Wickramasuriya is a former humanitarian worker turned software engineer. After harbouring a lifelong, secret desire to be a writer, Nayela has taken the plunge to write the book she has yearned to read but is yet to find. She is happiest exploring identity, community, and the vague sense that something greater is out there.

Judges' Quotes

On the Anthology

'A joy to discover these fresh voices in fiction. This collection of stories is exciting in range and originality, both in subject and form.'

Elise Dillsworth

'What a delight to read the entries for the Brick Lane Bookshop Short Story Prize. The longlist gave such diverse reading pleasures, yet every story, without exception, allowed me to enter worlds which felt carefully realised and full of possibility. As a short-story writer and reader, I don't need much convincing of the special power of the form, but these entries confirmed it once more – and most emphatically!'

Wendy Erskine

'I was struck by the breadth, ambition and flair of the stories in the prize. This anthology presents a thrilling sample of distinctive new talent at work today and highlights some exciting emerging writers for us all to follow.'

Kishani Widyaratna

1st Prize

Earth-Grown Bodies – Aoife Inman

'A well-drawn and poignant observation of the effects of a catastrophe on a community and a good sense of place.'

Elise Dillsworth

'This is a beautifully drawn story of power, complexity and nuance. A worthy winner.'

Wendy Erskine

'I really admired the humanity and pathos of Aoife Inman's story. A striking opening line intrigued me from the first page and I was enthralled by the story of this small community throughout. An assured new voice.'

Kishani Widyaratna

2nd Prize

WATCH AND SUBSCRIBE!! Artemisia eats entire Chicken Shop Menu – Mukbang LIVE! – Danielle Vrublevskis

'Original and bold story. Inventive in form, deftly written and comic touch nicely judged.'

Elise Dillsworth

'It was thrilling to read a story where a writer's daring in terms of structure is so successful. This is truly contemporary writing.'

Wendy Erskine

'A highly original and topical story with a distinctive, frenetic and funny voice. A bold new talent.'

Kishani Widyaratna

3rd Prize

Reputation Management – Katherine Gutierrez

'Fresh, engaging voice and assuredly written story. Lovely descriptive language and characters are nicely realised.'

Elise Dillsworth

'A funny, surprising and fresh story that had me right there in its world.'

Wendy Erskine

'I really enjoyed the slightly off-kilter dark humour and playfulness of this story. There's a lovely, unpredictable energy to it that made me want to see where this author would take me.'

Kishani Widyaratna

Shortlisted Stories

Details – Leeor Ohayon

'Sparse, evocatively written story about the dynamics of a relationship. Atmospheric setting.'

Elise Dillsworth

'This anatomy of a brief relationship was compelling and had a lovely ache to it.'

Wendy Erskine

'I enjoyed the wry political humour and fresh feeling of this story.'

Kishani Widyaratna

Donal – JP Pangilinan-O'Brien

'A good, perceptive account of domestic situations and nicely written.'

Elise Dillsworth

'This story is carefully paced and the characters precisely drawn. It was an utterly convincing rendering of particular individuals and the worlds they inhabit.'

Wendy Erskine

'The writing in "Donal" is spare but purposeful, considered and at times quite striking. I enjoyed the strong characterisation and affecting exploration of masculinity, adolescence and family secrets.'

Kishani Widyaratna

Sugar – Nayela Wickramasuriya

'Engagingly written and perceptive look at friendship between young girls and its costs, framed by their wider society.'

Elise Dillsworth

'This complex, deft tale of friendship was handled with care and dexterity.'

Wendy Erskine

'Captures the complications of friendships between young girls so well. The dramatic tension is tautly sustained and astutely judged.'

Kishani Widyaratna

Thanks

Every writer who entered this year's competition.

The fifty long-longlisted writers who made our job so enjoyable and difficult.

The twelve longlisted writers whose excellent stories make up this anthology.

First readers: Andrew Carson, Glenn Collins, Kalina Dimitrova, Chris Ellis, Andrew Everitt, Harry Gallon, Olivia Griffiths, Alison Hitchcock, Elinor Johns, Joe Johnson, Denise Jones, Jarred McGinnis, Kira McPherson, Pema Monaghan, Sophia Pearson, Rob Plinston, Tamara Pollock, Veena Sharma and Adelaide Turnbull.

Second readers: Xanthi Barker and Max Sydney Smith.

Judges: Elise Dillsworth, Wendy Erskine and Kishani Widyaratna.

Kalina Dimitrova for finance.

Denise Jones for her foreword.

All at Brick Lane Bookshop for believing in the competition and for their support.

Sue Tyley, our invaluable copy-editor.

Peter J. Coles and last year's winner Alice Haworth-Booth for making time to record a podcast.

Our stockists: Pages of Hackney, Burley Fisher Books, Libreria, Riverside Bookshop, No Alibis Bookstore, Rough Trade, Snap, Daunt Books and Broadway Bookshop.

Everyone who bought and read the 2019 and 2020 anthologies.

Friends and supporters on- and offline, including previous years' longlistees, Open Pen, Spread the Word, Comma Press, Republic of Consciousness Prize, MIROnline, Influx Press, *Sunday Times* Audible, and many others.

Online listings: writers-online.co.uk, nawe.co.uk, mironline.org, duotrope.com, neonbooks.org.uk, aerogrammestudio.com, christopherfielden.com, pocketmags.com, shortstoryaward.co.uk and nothingintherulebook.com.

Goodreads reviewers.

Clays printers.

Brick Lane Bookshop customers for their support.